P. K. Richer was born in Portsmouth, and attended Portchester Comprehensive School between 1980 and 1985. He left school with GCSE 'O' Levels in Art and English language, plus a handful of CSEs. He studied painting and sculpture at Portsmouth College of Art, performing arts at Southdowns College, and electronics servicing at Fareham College. He has also been a foundry worker, a sheet-metal worker, and a forklift truck driver.

For Mumsie, who taught me humanity

P. K. Richer

FROM SITZKRIEG TO BLITZKRIEG

AUSTIN MACAULEY PUBLISHERS™

LONDON • CAMBRIDGE • NEW YORK • SHARJAH

A CIP catalogue record for this title is available from the British Library.

ISBN 9781398419537 (Paperback)
ISBN 9781398419544 (ePub e-book)

www.austinmacauley.com

First Published 2023
Austin Macauley Publishers Ltd®
1 Canada Square
Canary Wharf
London
E14 5AA

Special thanks to Bev Rickard & Callum North, Brad Tuppen, Darren Coe, Graham Clarke, Jon Elson and everybody who smiled and nodded and said, "Yeah, that's good."

And, of course, to all my lovely loony family.

Introduction

When it was first suggested to me that I document some of my experiences during the Second World War, I was so thoroughly repulsed by the notion that I threw up all down myself. (The vast majority of my experiences around that time, you see, having been really rather shockingly painful and distressing.)

Who on Earth, I wondered, would be interested in reading about diarrhoea and vomit; near-starvation, traumatic amputations and whiffy pus; dogfights, machine guns and barbed wire; *or* those damned psychotic sausage-eating Nazis? (Nobody in their right mind, certainly!)

I had, of course, already published several autobiographical works by then: my earliest school years, at Westbury Grange, are detailed in *The Boy in the Blue Blazer*; and those 'difficult' times, which I spent at St Deferen's, Bagshott Manor and then Mandersby House, were committed to the page in *The Bounder*. The last work in the trilogy (and, by far, the most excruciating for me to undertake), *The Making of the Man*, documented my horrendously chaotic transformation, from a snot-nosed officer cadet at Letchworth Military Academy, to manhood proper, and my very first command.

All of this paled in comparison to the idea of recounting the horrendous events of the war years though. Indeed, the idea filled me with such an icy dread that I vomited again. The issue *did* continue to nag at me, however, and over time I began to allow a few of the less-hideous moments to filter-through from memory.

The years 1939 through 1945 were both terrifying and life-affirming. During that period, I made some of the very dearest chums that a chap could ever possibly have. (Unfortunately, I saw most of them either shot dead or blown to bloody pieces right before my eyes.)

The Diarist

I have, since the days of Westbury Grange, been an avid diarist and the volumes which I have accumulated over the years have proven to be extremely useful in filling-in some of the many gaping voids which now exist in my rapidly decaying mind. One diary entry which shall remain with me though (since it inspired the entire chapter 'The Peasant Auntie' in *The Making of the Man*) read:

Dear Diary,

I cannot believe it! The German chancellor looks like Charles Chaplin! I tripped over in the quad and jabbed myself in the eye with my pipe – and all in front of Cissy Frogmore-Mayweather. Bugger!

Colonel Gainsborough commended me on my steely resolve.

As language can change and evolve so rapidly, I intend to include a glossary of phrases and slang terms particular to the era. (Whether, or not, this shall make it into the first edition though, remains to be seen.)

It is for any readers who may be unfamiliar with my earlier works that I include this short 'about the author':

Tea

Tea is the very lifeblood of the British Army and of every true-hearted Englishman. (I am talking here of *proper* tea, mind you; not that awful green stuff which masquerades under the name in some of the more backward parts of the world.)

Tea is made from the leaves of the evergreen shrub, *Camellia sinensis*, of the family Theaceae. It is known to have been used in China since 2737 BC but was first brought to Europe around 1610 AD and remains, second only to water, the most frequently imbibed drink in the entire world. Only the tips (one bud plus the first pair of leaves) are picked from the bush, and proper tea undergoes an oxidation process which turns the green leaves to a dark brown or black colour – the longer the oxidation, the stronger and darker the brew. Popular varieties of black (or 'red') tea are: Assam, Nepal, Darjeeling, Nilgiri, Turkish and Ceylon.

The perfect cup of tea requires fine bone-china crockery and freshly drawn water. The pot should be warmed first (and always brought to the kettle – *never* the kettle to the pot) or else the temperature of the water can quickly fall below the critical value necessary for proper infusion to take place.

The strength of the tea is varied by adjusting the amount of leaves added to the pot and not its steeping time. Stronger teas, like Assam, are prepared with more leaves whilst those which are more delicate and high-grown, such as a Darjeeling, with somewhat fewer, as the more robust mid-flavours can sometimes overwhelm the subtle champagne notes. One slightly heaped teaspoon per person, plus one for the pot, is a very reasonable guide indeed. A black tea should steep for not less than thirty seconds and certainly no longer than five minutes. It is to be strained as it is served and only then should the milk be added.

Tea in bags *may* be resorted to in a survival situation (*if* it is a matter of tea or death) but the various so-called 'instant' teas which have been developed are base imitations – they are noxious and to be avoided at all costs. (The term 'herbal tea' is something of a misnomer since anything without camellia leaves is nothing more than an herbal *infusion*.)

My personal preference is for a good, strong Assam, brewed at 99° centigrade; steeped for three minutes and fifty-seven seconds and served in the very finest bone china; with just a dash of milk and two lumps of sugar.

Tobacco

It feels pertinent, at this juncture, to touch on my fondness for tobacco. I smoke cigarettes infrequently and cigars only on special occasions. I have not, however, since the age of twelve, been without a serviceable pipe of some kind (Barring a couple of tortuous nightmare episodes which we shall come to in due course).

The very best wood from which to fashion a tobacco pipe undoubtedly comes from the sweet briar *Rosa rubiginosa*, of the family Rosaceae. The burl at the base of its stem is extremely good at absorbing water (ensuring a supply for the briar through dry periods) and serves, in the finished article, to remove excess moisture from the smoke.

In my opinion (and, it must be said, that of most artisan pipe-makers), blocks cut from the heart of the burl (known as the *ebauchon*) make a very splendid pipe indeed, but those cut from the outer part (the *plateaux*), are far superior in terms of the beauty of their grain. (The other species in the genus is *Rosa canina*, the dog rose, and it is from these two that all of our cultivated roses are ultimately derived.)

On my sideboard at home (in a dark, Brazilian mahogany rack), I keep a treasured collection of lovingly handcrafted smoking implements. There are many briars; several of ebony and mahogany; and a long, slender-stemmed, cherry wood model, of which I am particularly fond. My favourite pipe of all though, is a large *calabash* (The type with which Sherlock Holmes is often associated – although mine is a good deal more enormous!).

Though I understand that calabash-style pipes, made from mahogany and other woods, may now be readily procured, these usually have a simple bore whereas the *true* calabash has a cooling chamber beneath the bowl. My own calabash is made (as all originally were) from a gourd. It has a deep meerschaum bowl (as opposed to one of porcelain) and a beautifully ornate ebony shank with a slim, flat mouthpiece and only a very slight lip.

'Calabash' is the name given to various vines of the family Cucurbitaceae, which includes the melon and pumpkin. More specifically, the name applies to the genus *Lagenaria*, of which the bottle gourd *Lagenaria siceraria* is the best known (rounder varieties are called calabash gourds). The calabash, whilst primarily grown not for food but for its use as a water container, was nevertheless one of the first cultivated plants in the world.

Somewhat confusingly, the name is shared with an evergreen tree *Crescentia cujete*, of the family Bignoniaceae, which is found in South America, India, and Africa, and which also produces gourds.

The leaves of *Nicotiana tabacum* (a broad-leaved flowering plant of the family Solanaceae) have long been smoked for the stimulant effect of the alkaloid substance *nicotine*. The process of curing the tobacco, however, was unknown amongst the native American smokers and, only when it was brought to Europe (poorly stored aboard ships) in the fifteenth century, did the practise become widespread.

The very gradual and incomplete drying of the tobacco leaves allows any harsh-tasting compounds to break down, which mellows and sweetens the finished product. The *true* art of producing outstanding premium tobaccos though, undoubtedly lies in the blending of the various and diverse elements. Three main varieties of *Nicotiana* are used: the Virginas are light, golden-yellow to yellow-brown in colour and are among the more mild in flavour whereas the Burley varieties tend to be a much darker (deep amber to rich chocolate-brown) colour and are of a stronger and more aromatic character. Finally, there are the Oriental spice tobaccos which are used, in more sparing quantities, to bring together the other elements and add different degrees of depth and richness to the final blend.

In years gone by, Mr Finch (my most excellent tobacconist) would knock up batches of a rich, dark blend of variously cured Burleys with a little light Virginia and just a few pinches of Oriental spice. It was known locally (when shredded most coarsely) as Finch's *Dark Bastard Shag*. It was a maverick and boisterous smoke which could induce, in even the most seasoned of pipe-smokers, cold sweats and nausea. Sadly, these days, I must settle for homogenised, mass-produced, commercial mulch like Gold Block, Condor or (God forbid) that Clan *silage*!

Nota bene: It seems that medical science has now established an irrefutable link between the smoking of tobacco and various potentially fatal maladies. Okay, so?

Now then…gin.

Gin

In the brewing world, malt is the grain of a cereal, such as barley, oats, or wheat etc., which has been allowed to germinate and is then dried in a kiln. Different rates and temperatures of drying are used to produce amber, brown, black, or pure malts. Malts may be fermented, to make beers or lager beers, but are put to far better use when fermented and then distilled to produce spirits such as gin. Gin is distilled from a fermented mash of wheat (*Triticum*), rye (*Secale cereale*), or maize (*Zea mays*), and flavoured with berries from the juniper (*Juniperus*).

In 1650, a Dutch physician, named Franciscus Sylvius, invented Dutch gin as a diuretic medicine and soldiers fighting in the Thirty Years' War began to use it for its warming effects on the body in cold weather (and for its settling effect on the nerves prior to battle). It was English soldiers, fighting in the Dutch Republic, who nicknamed the drink 'Dutch Courage' in reference to the potvaliancy that resulted from quaffing Dutch gin.

Following the Thirty Years' War, troops returned to England with the beverage and it was soon being distilled here. The gin which we were producing in England, though, was not the same as the original *Dutch gin* because English distillers did not possess the recipe. Dutch gin is the traditional liquor of the Netherlands and Belgium, from which gin evolved. The word 'gin' comes from the Dutch *jenever* ('juniper') – what the Frenchies call *genièvre*.

The drinking of gin became a good deal more popular in England after William III ('William of Orange') actively encouraged production by allowing unlicenced gin distillation whilst heavily taxing all imported spirits. Gin was sometimes even paid to workers as part of their wages.

In eighteenth-century Britain, the low price of corn led to such an epidemic of gin drinking that Parliament passed the Gin Acts of 1736 and 1751, successfully reducing consumption by 75%.

Gentlemen's Grooming

I feel that I should now also include a few words on the subject of moustaches. I am a fervent advocate of the wearing of facial hair (by a man, that is; ladies of hirsute disposition certainly ought not to go about public places with such in evidence).

The *English* moustache (parted in the middle and carefully waxed to the sides), is a very reasonable adornment for a chap's upper lip (provided it is not too sparse), as are the *Imperial* (similar to a *Horseshoe* but longer and swept outwards and upwards across the cheeks) and the *Walrus* (large and bushy, without a parting, and extending well below the lip). The standard *Chevron* is quite acceptable (as long as it is not trimmed too short) but silly little novelty styles like the *Pencil*, the *Toothbrush* and the *Fu-manchu* are not proper moustaches at all and should be quite beyond the consideration of anybody who is legally sane.

Myself, I am a wearer and avid devotee of the *Handlebar* moustache, and I believe that it represents the absolute pinnacle-of-perfection in conceptual moustache design. To me, it embodies all of the very finest principles in the cultivation and styling of upper-lip hair. The Handlebar requires careful nurturing and meticulous grooming and maintenance; and only with the very finest tools and styling-medium can one possibly hope to achieve such wondrous splendour. My own 'tache is exclusively maintained using the Deluxe Wilkinson Sword Gentleman's Grooming Set (comprising: a pearl-handled razor and strop; medium and small barber's scissors; a fine-toothed ivory comb; and a pair of ear-nostril-and-crevice pluckers, in sterling silver). My preferred styling-medium is Minge and Blackwood's Number 9 (firm-set) beard, moustache and eyebrow wax.

England

For foreign readers (whose tribes must have been living at the bottom of the Marianas Trench for the last forty-thousand years, if they do not already know), England is a green and pleasant land which forms the largest, most polite and well-dressed part of the United Kingdom of Great Britain.

England is, by far, the most beautiful and wonderful place in the entire world; Modern English is the richest, most elegant and refined, perfect language in existence; and English culture is, second to none, the oldest, most advanced and sophisticated, wonderful way for human beings to live that there has ever been. England is as close to Utopia (and to Heaven) as it is possible to come.

England is the country which used to run the world before America was invented.

After careful consideration (and quite a few glasses of gin) one evening, I decided that it may, after all, prove to be a worthy endeavour, per se, in which to engage at this, the twilight of my long and eventful life. I took my gin (and the bottle) into the study and seated myself at the desk in front of my battered old Imperial typewriter. I slipped a clean, crisp sheet of white foolscap into the machine, turned the roller until the top edge appeared behind the key-guide, and latched-on the 'Caps Lock' key. I drained my glass of its contents and poured myself another, stoked-up the old calabash, then began to tap away at the age-worn keys and produced the following:

THE ARDENNES, BELGIUM. MAY 1940.

I then fell asleep.

The Phoney War

That I should pursue a career in the army was, I suppose, somewhat inevitable; there has long been a tradition of military service in the family, of course, and readers who are familiar with my earlier autobiographical works will already be aware of my great propensity for fighting. My introduction to the art of war is well-enough documented in *The Making of the Man*, so I shall allude to it no further than relating that I graduated from Letchworth Military Academy, and received His Majesty's Commission, on April 24, 1929. Despite military schooling of the very highest order (without equal anywhere in the world, in my opinion), my introduction to the *reality* of war was…well, it was an eye-opener, to say the least: long periods of boredom, punctuated by moments of abject terror.

But let me not get ahead of myself…

In the decade leading up to the outbreak of open conflict with Nazi Germany, I spent a good deal of my time, when not honing my combat and command skills, attempting to beguile my way into young ladies' underwear. (I have, since the very first faint stirrings of early adolescence, been possessed of a particular penchant for comely young ladies and their underwear – and relished the challenge of separating the one from the other.) In the past I have been called 'The Bounder' and I cannot, in conscience, maintain that – at one time perhaps – the moniker was not thoroughly well earned. Anyway, my admittedly huge propensity for recreational dalliance aside...

In September 1938, the British prime minister, Neville Chamberlain, returned to England with a piece of paper – the Munich Agreement – an assurance from the German chancellor, Adolf Hitler, that he [Hitler] had no designs on further European territories following his recent annexation of Sudetenland. Chamberlain claimed that it would guarantee 'peace in our time' but it did not prevent Hitler from seizing the rest of Czechoslovakia in March 1939. Then, on August 25 that year, Adolf Hitler and Joseph Stalin signed a non-aggression treaty (the 'Hitler-Stalin pact' – negotiated by German foreign minister, Joachim von Ribbentrop, and his Russian counterpart, Vyacheslav Mikhailovich Molotov), which secretly made provision for the dividing-up of Poland between them if Germany should happen to invade that country. This, then, was all the security which Hitler needed and, on September 1, the blighter went and did just that. Britain and France, of course, promptly declared war on Germany and became embroiled in the six years of horrific and bloody conflict which came to be known as the 'Second World War'.

Out of the wireless set came Chamberlain's now famous sombre statement:

"I am speaking to you from the cabinet room of 10 Downing Street. This morning the British Ambassador in Berlin handed the German government the final note stating

that, unless we heard from them by 11 o'clock, that they were prepared at once to withdraw their troops from Poland, a state of war would exist between us. I have to tell you now that no such undertaking has been received and that consequently this country is at war with Germany."

There was little appetite on either side for any *immediate* engagement however, and the relative lack of action was such that the entire period came to be known as the 'Phoney War'. (Here in Blighty, that is; the sausage-eating Hun called it the *Sitzkrieg* or 'Sitting War'.) Eventually though, a new British Expeditionary Force (BEF) was to be deployed overseas to France – on which Hitler now had his beady little Nazi eyes firmly fixed. Preparations soon began and, in the spring of 1940, the 1st Halberdiers Regiment was duly mobilised.

Colonel Brompton was a heavyset, greying, veteran of the Great War, with a splendid imperial moustache and boisterous, unruly eyebrows. "We shall be shipping-out from Portsmouth," he informed me.

"Portsmouth, sir?" I frowned.

"Home of the Royal Navy apparently," he replied with a shrug. "Your barracks, in fact, are on the naval base – just around the corner from HMS *Victory*."

"Righty-ho then." I nodded. "Portsmouth it is, sir."

God, I could picture it all-too vividly: a tired, grey promenade along a pebbly beach; amusement arcades; fish and chips; and wall-to-wall bloody matelots! Still, I supposed that the city must have its share of fair young maidens who were in need of my immediate and most considered attentions. (This turned-out to be true enough, though I have to say that the quality of the breeding stock in 'Pompey' left an awful lot to be desired!)

Portsmouth

Portsmouth (or 'Pawts-muff' if you are a local), has a good deal in common with our nation's capital: both cities are squalid and filthy and have been so since time immemorial. The seafront at Southsea was just as I'd imagined: hotels and other large, residential buildings and shopfronts overlooked a wide swathe of common land, beyond which lay Clarence Esplanade, Southsea Castle, and along the beach to the east, the seaweed and barnacle-encrusted ironwork of South Parade Pier (with all of the usual garish seaside attractions) reaching out into the Solent. The area around the dockyards at Old Portsmouth was similarly as predicted: pre-Victorian, drab, grey, and crawling with prostitutes and bloody jolly Jack tars.

"Allo, darlin'!" a scraggy old hag called from a half-lit doorway. "Lookin' fer a good time, soldier?"

Yes, I thought to myself, *which is why I shall keep walking, thank you!*

I decided that a drinking establishment called 'The Ship' was probably as good a place as any to stop for a quick G&T on my way to the base. The door to the public bar swung closed behind me and I scanned the room, across a sea of navy blue, before striding up to the bar.

"Evening barkeep." I winked. "A gin and tonic, if you please."

"A word to the wise, if I may, sir?" said the gnarly old barman, as he set the glass down in front of me. "We don't get many soldiers frequent this 'ere establishment, sir. I think you'll find a good many more of yer chums up there in the town."

"Much obliged for that." I nodded. "I'll just have this one and be on my way."

(The keen-witted reader will doubtless have anticipated what subsequently came to pass.)

I finished my G&T and vacated the pub but noticed that the door opened again, shortly after. I'd not walked far when a voice called out from behind me. "Ooh, look lads; it's a *soldier-boy*," it squeaked. "One of them *Hablidiers* if I'm not mistaken!"

I glanced over my shoulder. "Get lost, you pansy tars!" I chuckled.

"Oy!" One of them yapped. "Me an' my shipmates take exception to that sort o' talk!"

I turned and took a quick gander about. "Perhaps you ought to go and fetch a few more of them then." I laughed. "It would seem that you girls are rather outnumbered."

One of the deluded sailor-boys revealed that he was in possession of a monkey fist. (A short length of rope, with a loop-handle spliced into one end, and a large, heavy, 'monkey-fist' knot tied in the other.) He began to swing it around his head in a manner which, I suppose, he thought would appear threatening.

"That's very pretty," I told him. "Do you do baton-twirling as well? You'd make a lovely majorette!"

28

He took a clumsy swing at me with the thing so I ducked underneath it and delivered a sharp jab to his solar plexus. (To my great amusement, the dozy skate wrapped the monkey-fist around his own neck and went straight to the ground with a loud, flatulent "Pffrt!")

I felt a fist prodding at me irritatingly in the cheek. (Much how it would feel, one imagined, were one to be struck in the chops by a little girl.) Whack! I brought my right elbow around sharply, at head-height, and *something* went crunch and squealed. I'd already seen the next damned fool winding-up for his turn; when he finally lumbered forward, he walked straight into one of the sweetest right hooks that I'd thrown in some time. 'Crack!' Went the bones in his face. "Aargh!" he shrieked. "He broke by bloody doze!"

Another little girl-fist came from somewhere behind me and caught me square in the kisser. I kicked out to my rear and the heel of my boot made contact with something which went 'squelch'.

"Ooaargh!" went the idiot behind me as he doubled-up on the deck.

There was hesitancy in the eyes of the next scrawny salt with whom I was confronted, so I gave him a swift sharp jab – right on the button – and he went down with claret gushing from his nose (and having done *nothing* whatsoever to defend himself!) Then came the sound of a lot of shuffling boots and, when I looked up, I realised that the rest of the ruddy spineless toads had scarpered!

I came away from the little fracas with a fat lip, a bruised right cheek, a swollen and discoloured left eye, and I felt splendid! I flashed my pass to the guard at Victory Gate and was duly admitted to His Majesty's naval base and dockyard.

I'd never seen so many ruddy matelots in all my life – the place was positively awash with salty seamen!

The following morning was clear and bright, with a few blobs of white, fluffy cumulus in the sky. I was mildly amused, when I went to report to Colonel Brompton, to see that the sailor standing on guard outside the building had a sticking plaster across the bridge of his nose and bruising under both eyes.

"Morning, seaman!" I smiled, as I flashed my pass. "Lovely day, eh?"

The stupid matelot glanced at my ID and then, with eyes fixed firmly forward, admitted me without uttering a word. I strode down a long corridor, looking right and left, until I found the colonel's office and was bid enter.

"I say, Hugo, what a splendid shiner!" Brompton exclaimed. "Are you back in the ring again then, my boy?"

"No, sir," I replied, shaking my head. "Last evening a couple of good-for-nothing sissy bluejackets thought that it might be good fun to bad-mouth the regiment, sir."

"Ooh dear." The colonel scowled. "The bloody fools!"

"Indeed, sir." I nodded. "Of course, I was obliged to teach the shirt-lifting blackguards some respect."

"Did any of them live?"

"I'm afraid so, sir; I was just getting warmed up when all five of the spineless blighters turned tail and fled!"

"Ho-ho-ho!" Brompton chuckled. "Ah well, never mind eh – we shall need a *few* live ones to sail the ships."

The colonel then talked me through what I already knew: that Jerry had invaded Denmark, Norway, the Netherlands, Belgium and Luxembourg; and that the Frenchies themselves now faced the threat of imminent invasion, and rather needed some *vertebrate* British soldiers to go over there and bail them out. "Have your lads ready to depart in twenty minutes," he said finally.

"Twenty minutes, sir?" I frowned.

"Twenty minutes," he repeated. "HMS *Credulous* sails in thirty. You're bound for Le Havre but, of course, that's strictly between you, me and Captain Pollock – until after you've left port."

"Captain Pollock, sir?" I laughed. "Is that really his name?"

"Oh yes; supreme irony for a salt, what?"

"Isn't it just!" I chuckled.

"I'm afraid that my own departure is pending somewhat more immediately," Brompton went on, "so I shall bid you *bon voyage* and I'll see you in the land of snails and runny cheese, what?"

"Right-ho, sir." I nodded.

"Good man, Hugo. That's all."

I stood to attention and saluted the colonel, then about turned and left the room. I strode back outside, past the dozy matelot with the broken nose, and went to rally the troops.

The platoon quickly fell in outside the barracks and I had Sergeant Harris stand the men at-ease.

"Good morning chaps," I said. "Now, Colonel Brompton has just informed me that we are to depart in thirty minutes..." (I was interrupted by whispered murmurings.)

"Quiet in the ranks!" Harris barked.

"Yes, thirty minutes." I nodded. "So you are to have your kit packed, and ready to go, in fifteen. That is all. Carry on,

Sergeant," And with that, I turned and marched-off to ready my own kit.

"On the order to 'fall out'," Harris bellowed, "you will double-away; assemble your kit; and 'ave your rifles ready for inspection! Parade…wait for it, Hawkins! Parade…fall-out!"

HMS Credulous

His Majesty's ship, *Credulous,* was a shabby-looking craft with peeling grey paintwork and rusty fittings. (She was, in fact, neither shipshape *or* Bristol fashion!) The hull was apparently water-tight at least. I did notice, however, that the waves were lapping well over the summer saltwater limit on the Plimsoll line.

The vessel eased-away from the quayside and coasted, slow-ahead, through the mouth of the harbour, out into the Solent. I stood on the aft deck, puffing on the old briar, and watched Portsdown Hill, the Isle of Wight, and then the rest of the South Coast, slowly recede into the distance. When (and if) I would see England again, I had no idea. (I sincerely hoped that I might though – it would be a truly horrible thing indeed if my very last memory of home was Portsmouth dockyard!)

Most of the chaps who were gathered there at the stern looked a little green-around-the-gills but Corporal Manning particularly so. "All right there, Manning?" I nodded.

"Nah, I feel bloody rotten, sir." He frowned. "I can't understand it; I ain't *never* been seasick before."

"Ah, but you were never sailing-off to war before though, eh?"

"No," he sighed, lowering his head.

"Don't you worry about it," I said, as I seated myself next to him. "We're all in the same boat here, you know."

He looked around. "Yes, sir." He smiled feebly. "Indeed we are."

"Ho-ho! There you go." I chuckled. "Humour in the face of adversity; that'll see you through!"

"I'm afraid the humour's fast evaporatin', sir."

"Well, Manning, you see all those poofy matelots, up there?" (I pointed towards the ship's bridge.)

"Yes, sir."

"I have it on very good authority that each and every one of 'em wears pink, frilly, ladies' underwear beneath his uniform."

Manning guffawed loudly and stared at me wide-eyed. "Ladies' underwear, sir?" he sniggered.

"*Pink, frilly*, ladies' underwear." I nodded. "Knickers *and* brassieres, mind you!"

"Oh, my life!" He chuckled.

"What's more, did you know that the captain of this vessel is named Pollock?"

"Pollock, sir?" Manning smirked. "Really? Captain Pollock?"

"Yep." I nodded. "You couldn't make it up, could you?"

"Where d'ya reckon we're goin' then?" Hawkins suddenly piped-up.

"France, ya bloody twit!" said Davenport.

"I know that! I mean *whereabouts*?"

"Oh, I dunno." Davenport shrugged. "D'*you* know where we're goin', sir?"

"France, you bloody twit!" I replied. (The others all laughed.) "No, but seriously; all I can tell you is that we'll be disembarking in Le Havre to rendezvous with Colonel Brompton. We shan't know any more until I receive our orders."

"Do the Froggies do fish and chips, sir?" asked Hawkins.

"They do something called *pommes frittes*," I told him, "which are a *bit* like chips but ever so thin; and very mean portions too, I hear. They have fishermen, of course, so I suppose that *some* Frenchies must eat fish; the majority of them though, prefer to dine upon amphibians' limbs and gastropod molluscs."

"What the 'ell are *gastrified bollocks*, sir?"

"Molluscs, Hawkins." I tutted, "Gastropod molluscs – just avoid anything that they call *l'escargot*."

Miggs's ginger brow furrowed. "Less cargo?" He frowned.

"Escargot," I said. "It's what *we* call 'snails'."

"They really do eat 'em then, sir?" Davenport grimaced. "I was hopin' that was just a stupid myth."

"No," I said, shaking my head, "Nope, they love 'em – breakfast, lunch *and* dinner."

"Eurgh! Tha's disgustin'!" Hawkins gagged. "Wot the 'ell's wrong wiv 'em? They 'ave *proper* grub don't they, sir? You know; bread and that?"

"Yes." I laughed. "They have bread, cheese, pastries and suchlike."

"Thank God for that," he sighed.

"Unfortunately, though, it's all made from snails."

"Bleurgh!" Hawkins retched as he vomited over the side. (He farted loudly too – "Pffrrrt!")

"That's it, lad!" I chuckled. "Better out than in, eh?"

"What about gin, sir?" asked Manning.

"What *about* gin?"

"Do the Frenchies 'ave it, sir?"

"Yes, certainly they do," I replied. "Holland's not far away, of course, and it was first distilled by the Dutch, you know."

"Was it, sir?"

"Yes, a seventeenth-century Dutch doctor invented gin as a diuretic medicine; it was used by soldiers fighting in the Thirty Years' War, for its warming effects on the body – and its calming effect on the nerves – and was nicknamed 'Dutch Courage' by British troops who brought it back with them from the Dutch Republic. The word 'gin' comes from the Dutch *jenever*; which is what they call juniper."

"Well, I never knew that, sir!" Manning marvelled.

"You do now." I winked.

"But, what's juniper?" Hawkins frowned gormlessly.

"It's a plant, you simpleton!" Davenport tutted.

"It's an aromatic evergreen shrub of the genus *Juniperus*," I told Hawkins, "which is related to the cypress genera, *Cupressus* and *Chamaecyparis*; of the family Cupressaceae. Juniper bushes are found throughout temperate regions and the berries are used to flavour gin."

"Oh, right." He nodded.

"So, *Hawk-eye*," said Miggs. "Who invented gin then, mate?"

Hawkins screwed his face up and scratched his head. "Erm, was it Cyprus?"

The others creased-up laughing but 'Hawk-eye' Hawkins didn't seem to care. (I suppose that such severely intellectually challenged dullards must grow accustomed to the interminable ribbing.)

The Royal Navy provided a meal at lunchtime and the menu indicated that it was to comprise shepherd's pie, followed by treacle pudding. What actually arrived from the galley though was an unidentifiable, grey sludge and I honestly couldn't tell, even after tasting, which was supposed to be the shepherd's pie and which was the alleged treacle pud. (I'd swear, in fact, that they were two blobs of exactly the same awful, stodgy muck.)

"How was your lunch, Sergeant?" I asked Harris when I went back out on deck.

"*Unbelievable*, sir," he grimaced. "I didn't even know what it was meant to be!"

"Hm. Mine too." I nodded. "Was everybody's like it?"

"No, sir," he replied, shaking his head, "some was even worse!"

"Bleurgh!" went Corporal Manning as he vomited over the rail. ("Pffrt!" his backside erupted.)

"Still not found the old sea-legs yet then, eh?" I frowned.

"This ain't seasickness, sir," he gasped. "This is...Bleurgh!" (He threw-up again.) "I'm *proper* ill, sir!" ("Pffllrrp!" his arse agreed.)

There did seem to be an excessive amount of vomiting going on – even given the circumstances; soldiers and sailors, alike, were leaning over the sides and spewing for all they were worth.

"Would you excuse me for a moment, sir?" asked Harris, as he turned away sharply and chundered hard. "Bleeuurgh!"

I was beginning to feel just a little nauseous myself by then so I told the chaps some lie (about having 'important business' to attend to) and nicked-off quick to find a quiet spot, somewhere out of the way.

"Pffrt!" went my backside as I leaned over the rail and hurled violently. (I'm afraid that I followed-through, too.)

There came a yell from the deck below. "Eurgh! Puke over the side, you dirty sod!"

I quickly turned around and, whistling nonchalantly to myself, shuffled-off in search of lavatorial facilities. Once securely ensconced within the privacy of one of the officer's conveniences, I plucked-up the courage to remove my trousers and inspect my underwear. "Heurp!" I retched. "Oh, God!" (I had soiled them horribly!)

I carefully removed the soggy, stinking pants and let them fall, with a "splosh", into the toilet. I flushed the loo but the damned, rotten, foetid, Y-fronts remained there, floating in the bowl. I left the cistern to re-fill (whilst I cleaned myself up and pulled my trousers back on) and then tried flushing again but still the awful, filthy smalls refused to be dismissed. When the cistern had re-filled a second time, I flushed once more and, thankfully, the horrendous, offensive pants were finally banished from my cringing sight.

With a livid scowl fixed firmly on my face (and a thousand grim thoughts running through my mind), I stamped-off to hear Captain Pollock's explanation.

The bridge on HMS *Credulous* was every bit as shabby and awful as the rest of the rotten vessel; peeling paint, rusted fittings and items of equipment which were held together with bits of electrical wire or gaffer tape appeared to be the norm. Captain Pollock was a lean, grey fellow with thin lips, mad white eyebrows, and crow's feet in the corners of his, slightly squiffy-looking, hazel eyes.

"Hello there." He smiled. "Poncenby is it? I'm told that you have a query, old chap?"

"No, Captain," I replied. "Fortunately *they* all seem to be in the navy."

"Huh-huh!" Pollock chuckled weakly. "There *is* something that you wanted to speak to me about though?"

"You're damned right there is!" I glared. "Why is it that there are so many sick men aboard this ship?"

Pollock nodded. "There *is* a lot of gippy tummy about isn't there?"

"Gippy tummy?" I exclaimed. "A gippy tummy is a bit of an unpleasant inconvenience; what's going on out there is bloody diabolical!"

"Mm. Yes, well, it does seem that hygiene procedures in the food preparation areas have become a bit lax of late," (There came a quiet "Pffrt!" from one of the bridge crew.)

"Lax sanitation?" I grimaced. "My god! Your galley must be disgusting!"

"To tell you the truth, I wouldn't know," he sighed. "I only took command of *Credulous* this morning. They told me that she was none too pretty or elegant but…"

"Well, don't you think that it might be a good idea to go and inspect it?"

"Oh, yes, absolutely," he agreed. "But not at the moment; the lower deck is flooded, I'm afraid."

"God, I knew that this bloody hulk wasn't seaworthy!" I glared. "Why are you not manning the lifeboats?"

"Relax; we're not taking-on water!" Pollock tutted. "There was a plumbing issue in the lavatories; a blockage, in the waste outlet, caused by a massive wad of soiled underpants."

"Don't you try to put the blame on us, Jack!" I told him. "Your *alleged* cook has poisoned most of my bloody men!"

"Yes, well, if it's any consolation at all, half of my crew have been affected as well."

"Aha! So the offending pants could well have been *theirs* then?" I scowled.

"Yes," said the captain, sighing again. "Look, let's not get caught-up in finger-pointing and recriminations about whose pants they were, eh? Would you like a drink?"

"Hmmm. Rum, is it?" I said, narrowing my eyes. "I don't know about that actually, Captain Pollock. I've heard that it's rum-drinking that turns you chaps queer!"

"I beg your pardon?"

"Before you know it, I'll be wearing flappy-trousers, singing sea-shanties, and dancing the ruddy hornpipe!"

"What?"

"Oh, dear me." I chuckled. "I'm just pulling your leg, Captain."

"Ah! Pongo humour, eh?"

"Yes." I nodded. "I'm afraid that it can be a little abstruse for those of a nautical bent; what with it being so sparklingly epigrammatic and all."

"Hmmm?"

"No, it would be rude of me to refuse your grog, Captain. Most gracious of you, old chap."

(Rum may be a bit of a poofy matelot's drink but a couple of large ones certainly helped to blur the edges of reality a bit.) "Ho-ho-ho!" Pollock chuckled, wiping a tear from his eye. "*Gastrified* ones eh?"

"Mm-hm." I nodded. "Less cargo!"

I left the captain to carry out his duties up on his shabby bridge and descended the steep, rusting, iron stairs to find the larger part of my platoon gathered on the fore deck, frowning at a narrow strip of turquoise on the horizon.

"Land ahoy, sir!" said Harris, pointing.

"Mm. Soon be there now." I nodded.

"Sir?" said Davenport. "You got a moment, sir?"

"Yes, of course." I smiled. "What can I do for you, Private?"

"I've told Hawk-eye, here, that the ship's captain can't possibly be called 'Bollock', sir, but he insists that he is."

"Tha's what you told the corporal, wasn't it, sir?" Hawkins jabbered.

"No, his name's *Pollock*." I tutted. "You know; like the marine fish, *Pollachius*, of the cod family?"

"Captain Bollock, indeed!" Davenport chuckled, nudging Hawkins with his elbow. "You daft bugger!"

"What *is* it with you and gonads, Hawk-eye?" I asked, eyeing him suspiciously.

"Go-nads, sir?"

"Bollocks, lad!"

"Fair enough, sir." He shrugged, looking down at the floor. "Sorry, sir."

(Any attempt at elucidation would have been utterly futile so I left it at that and turned to Davenport instead.) "I've heard a couple of the lads call you 'Tricky'," I said. "How did you come to earn such a nickname?"

"I can't really remember how it started, sir." He shrugged. "It used to be '*Tricky Nicky*'; my name bein' Nicholas."

"Ah." I nodded. "I once knew a *girl* called Nicholas, you know."

"Funny name fer a bird innit, sir?"

"Oh, her real name was Henrietta," I replied, with a wry smile. "It was due to her wanton promiscuity that everybody called her *knicker-less*."

The lads had a good old laugh – all bar one; a Brummie private named Hinckley.

"Why'd they call 'er that then, sir?" asked Hinckley. "Nicholas?" (The others chuckled all the more heartily.)

"Well, she was incredibly free-and-easy with her favours," I said, winking theatrically. "And so they called her – knicker-less."

Hinckley shrugged. "I don't geddit." (There was much sniggering amongst the other lads.)

"Oh, come on!" I tutted. "Say it to yourself, man – 'knickerless'."

"Nicholas," he said again. "… I still don't geddit!"

The others were rolling-around in stitches by then. Hinckley shook his head, frowned, and continued to puff on his Woodbine.

Curiosity got the better of me and I called Hawk-eye over to me. "Hawkins," I said. "Would you please tell me, quietly, why you think it was that we called the young lady Nicholas?"

"Well, sir; 'cos she couldn't keep 'er undies on, like? Or didn't even *wear* any!"

"Good." I smiled. "Thank you, Private; that'll be all."

Corporal Manning suddenly came marching around the corner wearing a deep frown. "Sir." He sighed, "Fidget and Wonky say that they've looked all over and they can't find Tubby anywhere."

"Okay, Corporal." I nodded. "Firstly, who the hell are Fidget and Wonky?"

"Sorry, sir; that's Ferguson and Warwick," he replied, gesturing with a thumb over his shoulder.

"And Tubby?"

"Tucker, sir."

"Right, so, let's just recapitulate," I said. "We have 'Hawk-eye' Hawkins, 'Tubby' Tucker, 'Fidget' Ferguson and 'Wonky' Warwick." I paused and gave a frown. "Hawk-eye, Tubby, Fidget, and Wonky? Christ; it sounds like the Seven Dwarves' destitute hillbilly cousins!" (There came cries of "Man overboard!" and *Credulous* began to slow.) "I would hazard a guess that old Tubby has been sighted!" I sighed.

Tucker was too far behind to hurl a life-preserver and so one of the lifeboats had to be launched and two tars rowed-out to retrieve the hapless, doggy-paddling private.

"How the bloody hell did you manage that?" I glared as Tubby stood there, with a blanket around him, shivering and dripping all over the deck.

"I was r-running to throw-up over the s-side, sir," he stammered, "and I s-slipped in someone else's s-sick and went straight over the r-rail!"

"Well, you'd better get yourself dried-out and warmed-up," I told him. "Sa'nt Harris, give this man a measure of gin."

"Yes, sir."

"Oh, th-thank you, sir!" Tucker nodded.

"And, before anybody gets any bright ideas," I said loudly, "nobody is going to get extra gin by throwing himself into the sea – Miggs, get down from there!"

Eventually (and after a good many more gallons of vomit had been ejected over the side), we arrived at the port of Le Havre. *Credulous* met the quayside with an almighty thud and there was a commotion and raised voices up on the bridge.

Once properly docked, we all began to file down the rickety gangplanks and Captain Pollock came down to check the bow of his ship, and the quay, for damage.

"Here, Poncenby, tuck this away somewhere, old chap," he said, handing me a bottle of brown stuff with an iffy-looking seventeenth-century buccaneer on the label.

"Rum?" I said, narrowing my eyes.

"A gesture of good will." He smiled. "It's top-notch stuff, you know – none of your cheap rotten grog."

"Well, that's very considerate of you, Captain. It'll probably make a decent Molotov or something, eh?"

Pollock's chin nearly hit the toe of his boot.

"No," he gasped. "It's really *very* good."

"But I jest, sir." I laughed, slipping the bottle into my pocket.

"Oh, thank goodness for that," he sighed.

"Yes." I winked. "I shall need to keep this for fire-lighting."

Le Havre

Such demand was there for the lavatories that it was necessary to divide the platoon into a number of *sittings*. I then did a quick headcount before marching the chaps across the port, to our supply depot, where I found Colonel Brompton bustling around in an office near the gate.

"Ah, Hugo, m'boy!" He smiled. "How was the crossing? I heard that you had a man overboard."

"Ugh! Tucker, sir." I nodded. "In his haste to disgorge himself over the side, he slipped in somebody else's chunderings and flew straight over the bloody rail!"

"Ho-ho-ho!" Brompton chuckled. "The silly bugger! Did you make him swim the rest of the way?"

"I would've done, sir." I shrugged. "But some tars rowed-out and fetched him back on board so, short of throwing the daft sod back in again…"

Conversation, however, quickly turned to matters of an altogether more cheerless and forbidding nature and the colonel drew my attention to a large-scale map of Belgium; one of many such maps which were pinned to the walls about the place. "We appear to have reached somewhat of an impasse on the northern lowlands," he said, prodding at Antwerp and Brussels with his baton. "The whole thing has settled into something rather disturbingly reminiscent of the last war and no real gains are now being made by either side."

"Hm," I mused. "So, if Jerry can't pull-off a Schlieffen Plan manoeuvre, what's his next move going to be?"

"Well now, the Hun, as we know, is a wily beggar," Brompton scowled, "And you can bet your bottom that he'll try *any* low-down and underhanded skulduggery which he thinks will enable him to bring his filthy panzers rumbling into rural France."

"So he'll be looking to establish a bridgehead across the river Meuse, eh?"

"Exactly." The colonel nodded. "The latest intelligence reports suggest that the thrust of any attack will likely be concentrated somewhere between Namur and Dinant." (He waggled his baton up and down the Meuse.) "I want you to take your platoon and report to General Allcock, in Valenciennes," he continued, stabbing at the map on the French side of the border. "The general will have much more detailed and up-to-date information for you and will direct you to where you'll be needed."

"Right-ho, sir."

"Well, now, I've begged and pleaded with the chief of staff," Brompton went on, "but I was told, in no uncertain terms, that there are no armoured personnel carriers available. I did, however, manage to commandeer for you a couple of trucks; the Boys anti-tank guns, which you asked for; and a couple of extra LMGs." (LMG = Light Machine Gun.)

"Jolly good, sir," I said. "I was wondering, though, about the gin situation."

"God, you're not depleted already, surely?" The colonel frowned.

"No, sir," I replied, shaking my head, "but what we have won't last more than a couple of days."

"Alas, *everything* is in short supply, Hugo," he sighed. "Just do what you can, my boy."

"Yes, sir." I nodded, sighing forlornly. "Oh, I shall need to requisition some items of clothing also, sir."

"But all you've done is crossed the bloody Channel!" Brompton exclaimed. "Why on earth would you need to be issued with new uniforms already?"

"It's not so much uniforms as underwear, sir. I'm afraid that most of the platoon are suffering from the effects of the Navy's rotten catering and sanitary practises and have succumbed to a variety of severe gastrointestinal maladies."

"My God, they've all got the trots?"

"The screaming bloody hab-dabs, sir," I replied. "They should have named that damned ship *Insalubrious*!"

I returned to the platoon and led them to the motor pool, where our transport awaited: two Commer Q4s and a Ford F2. All three of the battered, rusty, old trucks had seen better days and the chaps' reaction to them was understandably subdued. (The Ford was the least shabby of the vehicles so I made that my 'gin palace'.)

While food, fuel, ammunition and other supplies were being loaded, I thought that a little pep-talk might be in order. "All right now chaps," I said. "The importance of our mission here cannot be overstated. What is at stake is no less than the future freedom of the whole of Western Europe – perhaps the entire world!" (I was seeing a lot of anxious frowns so I changed tack.) "Let us endeavour though, to keep our spirits high, eh? And show these awful, spineless, continental types how British soldiers conduct themselves in battle." (The reaction was still rather underwhelming.) "Oh, and, by the way," I added, "I just stopped-in at the quartermaster's store and requisitioned three-dozen brand new pairs of underpants."

"Oh, good show, sir!" Manning exclaimed, accompanied by a chorus of approving cries.

"Issue pants to those men who require them, Sergeant," I told Harris.

"Yessah!" He nodded.

"And then, I think, divvy-up the gin ration, eh?"

"Gin!" the lads all cheered. "Hurrah!"

"May we smoke, sir?" asked Miggs.

"I rather think that we *should*." I nodded as I loaded-up the old briar.

While the lads had a smoke and a drink and a chinwag, I had a quick word with my sergeant.

"Look, Harris," I said quietly. "I want you to keep this under your hat, old boy, but I'm afraid that the only gin we have, at the moment, is that which we brought with us."

"Oh my God!" he gasped, a smouldering Capstan dangling from his bottom lip.

"All right now, keep it down, eh?" I told him. "We have enough, for the time being, but it's not going to last for long."

"And what are we to do when it's gone, sir?" he asked, taking the ciggie from his mouth.

"I don't know, Sergeant," I sighed gravely. "I'm afraid that I just... I really don't know."

The gin ration having been had, we mounted-up and were soon trundling through the filthy, rotten, smelly, ugly streets of Le Havre, en-route to Amiens on the river Somme. For the first leg of the journey, I had Sergeant Harris take the lead, in the first of the Commers; Manning followed him, in the second; and I played back-marker, in the Ford, so that I could keep an eye on everyone else. By then, the cloud had thickened to form a low, rolling, and stratocumulus mass but held the promise of little more than some light showers.

All of France is completely awful. (Picturesque it may be – in *tiny* parts – but it is also crawling with coarse, vulgar Frenchies.)

We had not been on the road for long before we found ourselves passing through Bolbec and there came a strong whiff of garlic and stale urine from an old, toothless, yokel – with scruffy, baggy trousers hanging on red braces – who called out to us as we passed by. (It is a damning indictment of the French psyche, incidentally, that their spoken language requires the making of such *revolting* noises!)

"Bravo! Vive la Grande Bretagne!" He drawled. *"Formidable, messieurs!"*

"Not too bad, thanks!" I nodded. "Seen any Jerries hereabouts?"

"Erm... *Je ne parlez l'Anglaise,*" said the crusty old Frog.

"That's right; we're here to give the wily Hun a ruddy good pasting," I told him.

"Je ne comprend pas, monsieur." He shrugged.

"Smashing!" I smiled. "We'll soon give the Boche what-for, eh? Toodle-hoo!"

"Au revoir," the shabby bumpkin waved. (Bloody Frenchies – would it be too much trouble for them to have the occasional wash and learn some damned English?)

We'd only travelled another fifteen miles or so when I noticed that the lead vehicle was leaving a trail of orange sparks in the road in its wake so I signalled everybody to halt. There was a loud "BANG!" as Manning slammed his Q4 right into the back of Harris's. Sergeant Harris leapt from his cab scowling. "Manning!" he seethed. "I thought you said you could drive!"

"Sorry, Sarge." Manning frowned. "But you ain't got no brake lights."

"You knew that we were stoppin' though?"

"Yeah, but the brakes on this thing are bleedin' crap!"

"In fairness, Sergeant, the brakes on the old gin palace are a bit...*crap*, too," I said. "I nearly rear-ended Manning myself – and he *does* have brake lights."

"Why have we stopped then, sir?" asked Harris.

"Because your ruddy exhaust is hanging-off, old boy."

Harris cast an eye beneath the truck. "Oh yeah." He tutted. "The bloody bracket's rusted-through."

"Can we get out and stretch our legs please, sir?" asked Wonky Warwick.

"Yes," I replied. "Everyone dismount and have a bit of a stretch. Smoke if you've got 'em."

"Whassup wiv Gertie then?" asked Hawk-eye.

"Gertie?" I frowned.

"Oh, the lads have named our wagon 'Gertrude', sir," Harris explained. He turned to Hawkins. "Nothing serious, lad," he told him. "Just a loose exhaust."

"Huh, we named ours too," said Manning. "She's called 'Bertha'."

"Right, okay." I nodded. "So what do you think that we ought to call the gin palace, then?"

"How about 'Ginny', sir?" Warwick suggested.

"Hm," I mused. "Somehow she just doesn't look like a Ginny to me."

"What about 'Steven' then, sir?" Hawkins babbled.

"Don't be daft, lad; it has to be a *girl*'s name." I tutted. (*"Dullard!"*)

"How about 'Nelly', sir?" Harris offered. "I think she looks like a Nelly."

"Mm. Yes, I think she *does* looks a bit like a Nelly, you know."

Manning held Gertrude's rusty, decrepit exhaust in place while Harris fixed it there with some brass wire.

"Why *is* it that we always call boats an' cars an' that '*she*', sir?" Davenport asked.

"I believe it stems from the fact that only females *carry*," I told him.

"Oh, right," he said. "Yeah, that makes sense."

"Except for seahorses, that is," I added, as an afterthought.

"Seahorses, sir?"

"Yes, there are several genera but *Hippocampus* is typical. In seahorses, it is the *males* that carry the offspring."

"Well, I never knew that!" Davenport exclaimed.

"You do now though, eh?"

"Job's a good 'un, sir," Harris reported. "That'll hold – 'til the chassis rusts through, anyway."

"God!" I frowned. "And how long before that's likely to happen?"

Very deliberately, and wearing a wry grin, Harris checked his wristwatch. "Well, she *might* make it to Amiens, sir." He winked.

"Strewth!" I chuckled. "Let's get ready to move out then. I shall take the lead this time and I'm afraid that Gertrude is going to have to be back-marker. Let's leave ourselves a bit more stopping distance too, eh?"

The Somme

We continued to trundle eastwards across France without any major incident and had reached Amiens by teatime so we halted there, brewed-up some char and ate some rations. The sky was decidedly grey and overcast and a little drizzle had begun to fall. (The food and the tea, I remember, were both piss-poor.)

I instructed Harris and Manning to give all three of the trucks a quick once-over and list any significant faults which they came across. The two of them spent about half an hour on the task before coming to report their findings.

"Let's start with old Gertie then, Sergeant," I told Harris. "What's the score there?"

"Well, sir, her tyres are very badly worn," he replied. "As are the brake pads and the clutch; the speedo doesn't work; and, of course, we already know about the exhaust bracket and the brake lights."

"I suppose it could be worse." I shrugged. "How about Bertha?"

"Much the same, sir; the tyres, clutch and brakes are all on the limit; the front and rear left indicators are not working and nor is the horn. Her steering's a bit on the slack side too."

"And Nelly?"

"Well, sir, she's got no obvious electrical faults but, as you're doubtless already aware, her brakes, clutch and tyres are all rubbish."

"Mm." I nodded. "Right-ho, thank you, Sergeant. You two come and have some char, eh."

Harris and Manning re-joined the rest of us and we began to reflect on our surroundings.

"It beggars belief don't it, sir," said Harris, sipping his tea, "that so many of our brave chaps came over and fought the Jerries, here on the Somme, in the Great War? And now we're back here to have-it-out with the blighters once again."

"Hmmm," I sighed. "The swine have got a bloody nerve all right."

"The war to end all wars?" Harris scowled. "Huh!"

"What kicked all *that* off then, sir?" asked Tucker.

"In a word," I said, "bloody Serbia! I realise that was *two* words, of course…"

"Serbia, sir?"

"Yes, *'tiresome Serbia'* in Queen Mary's words; Austria-Hungary, Franz Ferdinand and the King of Prussia – Kaiser bloody Wilhelm!"

"I'm not sure that I follow you, sir." Tubby frowned.

"Oh, it's a long and tedious story," I told him. "Basically, some Serb nationalists assassinated the archduke of Austria; the German Kaiser approved a ridiculous Austrian ultimatum to the Serbs, and Russia – the protector of Slavs – mobilised against Austria. Germany then declared war on Russia and France and promptly trampled all-over Belgium's neutrality to have a go at the Frenchies. Well, of course, we were then duty-bound to declare war on Germany and about ten million people ended-up dead."

"Blimey!" said Warwick. "Ten million dead 'cos of one bloke?"

"Mm." I frowned. "Pretty much."

"Me dad was over 'ere, back then," said Manning. "In the Battle of the Somme."

"Ah, yes." I nodded. "He was with the Halberds too, wasn't he?"

"Yeah, that's right, sir. It's funny though; he must've seen all sorts of stuff but he never talks about it."

"Hmmm. It's the same with a lot of those veterans, I think. They don't like to discuss it. Who can blame 'em, eh?"

"My old dad never came back." Harris shrugged. "He's still over here; in one of these fields somewhere."

"It's thanks to chaps like him though," I said. "That the battle, here in Amiens in 1918, marked the beginning of an offensive which eventually saw the Boche driven-back and defeated."

"Was *you* here in the Great War then, sir?" asked Hawkins.

"Bloody hell, Hawk-eye!" I gasped. "How sodding old do you think I *am*, lad?"

"Well, I dunno, sir…"

"Christ! I was four years old when it started!"

"It was *that* long ago then?"

"Given that I was born in 1910, Hawkins, and that it is now 1940, how old am I?"

Hawk-eye scratched his witless head. "Erm, is it fifty, sir?"

"Fifty?" I exclaimed. "Do I *look* like I'm bloody fifty?"

"No, not really, sir."

"You arrived at that figure by adding up ten and forty, didn't you?"

"Yes, sir." He nodded.

"Strewth!" I chuckled. "Time to break-out the gin, I think, Sergeant."

"Yessah!" said Harris.

"Hurrah!" the lads cheered.

"Old Prince Albert; he was a Jerry wasn't he, sir?" asked Davenport.

"Mm." I nodded. "Yes, he was the second son of Ernest, Duke of Saxe-Coburg-Gotha. As well as being Queen Victoria's husband, Albert was also her first cousin."

"Eurgh! That's in-sexed though innit?" Hawkins gabbled. (I stared at him in wonder.)

"You mean *incest*." Miggs laughed.

"Yeah, *that*. It is though innit, sir?"

"Well." I shrugged. "I mean, not *strictly* speaking…bloody nearly!"

"Why *do* them Jerries 'ave t' go around makin' such a soddin' nuisance of 'emselves?" Tucker scowled.

"Too much sausage and fermented cabbage in their diet, lad," I told him.

"Fermented cabbage, sir?"

"Mm. That's what that sauerkraut muck is, you know; ruddy fermented cabbage!"

"Eurgh! Is it?" he grimaced. "Well, I never knew that!"

"You do now, eh." I winked. "No, but Jerry was destitute after the last war, you see; he was required to pay huge reparations for all the damage caused, and sackfuls of his money became worthless. The German nation – which still harboured lofty aspirations of imperial greatness – found itself on its knees, humiliated in defeat. Well, I'm afraid that, out of desperation, they have delivered supreme executive power into the hands of a ruddy criminal madman."

"Criminal madman, sir?" Warwick exclaimed.

"Absolutely." I scowled. "Make no mistake, Hitler's ideology and philosophy are bloody chilling; he has this idea that there is a blonde-haired, blue-eyed, Aryan, master race and that all other colours and creeds are inferior thereto. The Nazis have a state-sponsored bloody eugenics breeding programme for God's sake! Under their so-called national socialism, the individual is afforded no rights whatsoever in their dealings with the State, and even the most basic of liberties, which we currently enjoy, would be denied us. Enslavement is their game."

"What a bunch o' complete bastards!" Manning glared.

"Yes." I nodded. "And that, my lads, is why the Nazis simply *must* be stopped – whatever the cost may be!"

"Oh, it's the river *Somme*!" Hawk-eye suddenly exclaimed, squinting at a map. "I always thought it was the *Song*."

"You bloody twit!" Davenport sniggered.

"The Battle of the Song?" Sergeant Harris chuckled. "Oh, Hawkins, you daft 'apeth!"

The lads all had a good chuckle but old Hawk-eye, as ever, just shrugged it off.

"We'd probably best get a jaldi on, if we're gonna be there on time, sir," Harris suggested.

"Yes." I nodded, checking my watch. "Quite right, Sergeant. Come on then, chaps; let's mount-up."

We'd trundled onwards for another sixty miles or so, and were just outside of Arras, when Bertha began to lurch and splutter and then juddered to a halt.

"She just started dying, sir," said Manning, climbing down from the cab.

"Are you low on fuel?" I asked him.

He shrugged. "A little bit perhaps, but she *can't* be empty, sir."

"But, if the fuel's low, some muck's probably been dragged up from the bottom of the tank and caused a blockage."

"Oh, yeah; I bet that's it, sir!"

"Okay, everyone," I said, "we might as well dismount for a bit."

"Ooh, sir, 'ave I got time to go and 'ave a bit of a clear-out, like?" asked Hawkins.

"Mm." I nodded. "Go across the road, in the ditch or something, but be quick, eh?"

"Yes, sir."

Although he'd gone a reasonable distance away, we all heard Hawk-eye's backside erupt with a "PFFRRPLLRRP!" and the lads all fell-about.

"No blockage *there* then, eh?" I laughed.

Harris was an absolute whiz with vehicle maintenance and mechanics and had Bertha's fuel flowing again in no time. "All done, sir," he reported. "I've filled her up, too. Best we keep 'em all topped-up regular, I think."

"Good man, Sergeant." I nodded. "Two men – Miggs and Davenport – get a jerry can each and top-up Gertrude and Nelly."

"Yes, sir." They both nodded.

"All right, Hawk-eye?" I smirked as he came trudging back. "Is that better, lad?"

"Ooh, I've still got a bit of a poorly tummy, sir," he groaned.

"Yes, you have." I nodded. "That sounded extraordinarily unpleasant."

"It was, sir." He frowned. "It ain't 'alf made me arse sore too."

(It was then that I caught a whiff of the fearsome stench which had returned with Hawkins.) "Eurgh!" I retched. "For God's sake get downwind of us, man! Strewth!"

"Sorry, sir," he said, "but I wasn't quick enough and I'd already done a little bit in my pants before I got there."

"And you're still wearing them?" I gasped.

"Well, erm…"

"Eurgh! God!" I cringed, retching again. "Go and remove and discard them – at once!"

"Yes, sir."

"Sergeant; issue Private Hawkins with some fresh underwear, would you?"

"Yessah!" said Harris, holding his nose. "Away and clean yourself up then, Hawk-eye. On-the-double, lad! Jaldi!"

Hawkins carried-out some impromptu ablutions and we were soon under way again.

About an hour later – when we were only a couple of miles short of Valenciennes – a spotty, hairy, white arse suddenly poked out of Bertha's rear and started laying-down a trail of vile, runny faeces in the road. My stomach heaved violently and I threw-up all over the dashboard.

The bloody wind then gusted strongly and a sheet of the noxious yellow-brown diarrhoea splashed right across Nelly's windscreen, totally obscuring my view. I flicked the wipers on but, at first, the blades just smeared the awful, fluid excreta evenly across the glass; causing me to vomit again. Without thinking, just for one moment, I stuck my head out of the window, to better see where I was going, and my face was spattered and speckled with some dirty bugger's fetid arse-gravy. "Heurp!" I retched as I spewed all down my right arm.

CRUNCH! (I suddenly slammed Nelly into the back of Bertha.) "Bloody hell!" I seethed. (Harris then drove Gertie straight into the back of Nelly – BANG!) "Oh, for Christ's sake!"

I wiped the splatter from my face, and discarded the soiled handkerchief at the roadside, as I clambered down from the cab. "Right, dismount!" I yelled. "Everybody out!"

"I 'ad to slow down for the corner, sir," said Manning. "Are *my* brake lights kaput an' all now?"

"I don't know," I glowered. "I couldn't see a bloody thing through the disgusting filth on my windscreen!"

"Eurgh!" Manning gagged at the unspeakable muck all over Nelly's front end. "Heurp!"

"Who was it that dangled their rotten backside out of that vehicle and defecated over my gin palace?" I demanded. "Was it you, Hawk-eye?"

"No, sir, it weren't me!" he squeaked.

"Sorry, sir; it was me," Ferguson quailed. "I was desperate, sir; I didn't know what else to do!"

"Each of the vehicles has a designated emergency bucket; to be used if anybody needs a clear-out whilst we are in transit."

"Yeah, I know, sir, but Sanderson was on it."

"He was gonna do it in 'is tin hat, sir!" Warwick grimaced.

"Fidget!" Harris glared. "You dirty bugger!"

"You just lost your gin ration for the rest of the day!" I told Fidget. "You're a disgrace to the bloody regiment! Now, go and fetch some water, and a cloth, and clean off that horrible mess, whilst the rest of us point at you and laugh."

"Yes, sir," Ferguson cowered.

"Jaldi then!" Harris roared. "On-the-double!"

"Smoke-up, lads," I told the rest of the platoon.

"Erm, may I have permission to go for a clear-out, sir?" Asked Miggs.

"Yes, anyone that needs a bit of a clear-out may do so," I said. "Well-away from the vehicles though, eh?"

Being a man of my word, the rest of us pointed and laughed at Fidget as he began to sponge-down Nelly's front-end, retching constantly and occasionally gagging so hard that he puked. When all of the nasty filth had been washed away, I made him 'slop-out' the latrine buckets before we mounted-up and moved out again.

Valenciennes

Onward our little convoy trundled until we arrived in Valenciennes. Though there were still some scattered showers about, much of the cloud had begun to dissipate by then, promising a clear and chilly night. Valenciennes was filthy, stinking, and irretrievably shabby and ghastly – even by French standards.

"General Allcock, sir?" I said, saluting. "I'm Poncenby, sir; First Halberds."

"You should have been here an hour ago, Captain!" said Allcock, sniffing suspiciously.

(I wanted to say *"Why? What happened?"* but I didn't.) "Yes, my sincerest apologies, sir," I replied. "I'm afraid that we've had to contend with a multitude of minor mechanical malfunctions and the most messy of medical maladies."

"Yes, yes, all right," the general sneered. "All of that alliteration is making me giddy!"

"Sorry, sir." I frowned. "I didn't realise that I was doing it."

The general then proceeded to expound the virtues of the cavalry charge and talked of breaking-through the enemy line *'with sword and lance'*. (I gazed at him, in despairing disbelief, but said nothing.)

"Well now, I'm going to send you to Dinant, I think," Allcock said finally. "The chaps down there have been crying-out for reinforcements and, though I do have a company assigned, they may not arrive for a day or two. You'll go and lend whatever assistance is necessary to hold back the Hun, until those reinforcements arrive. Clear?"

"Crystal-clear, sir."

"Good man." Allcock beamed. "Jolly good show!" (He then went on to destroy any vestige of optimism that I may have still been harbouring.) "Now, a lot of chaps seem to explode when they come under fire – especially from heavy artillery and mortars – so try not to do that, won't you? I'm sure you can appreciate that it's not at all helpful."

"No, sir. Quite," (I was beginning to see that General Allcock was, possibly, just a little detached from reality.)

"Keep an eye out for troglodytes too," he went on.

"Troglodytes, sir?" I frowned, narrowing my eyes.

"Yes, they live in tunnels under the mountains…"

"Ri-i-ight," I sighed. (*'Oh God, he's mad!'*)

"… They're cave-dwellers, you know; forever digging. Always that infernal digging!"

"Yes, sir." (*'Mad as a bloody hatter!'*)

"And watch out for Jerry's pinzers too."

"Erm…do you mean panzers, sir?"

"No, *pinzers*; they have these great big pinzers on the ends of their arms," he said, gesticulating with his hands held like lobster claws.

(I closed my eyes while they rolled around in their sockets.) "Right-ho, sir." I nodded.

"Now, the rain looks like it will hold-off, so I'd bat first if I were you."

"Yep."

"Nanny says there will be no cake for cry-babies…"

"Mm-hm."

"…and don't chew your shoelaces!"

"Absolutely, sir!"

"Good. And, whatever you do, don't try to fire any of your lads out of a cannon; even for a laugh. It always ends badly. Trust me – I *know*."

"Got that, sir." I nodded. "No human cannonballs."

The general then handed me a shilling. "Slip this into your little pocket." He winked. "And then off you jolly well toddle, you young scamp!"

"Gladly, sir," I said, sighing deeply. (I left the general's office feeling more despondent than I had done since…well, more than I had done in a *long* while anyway.)

"Captain Poncenby?" A voice called out.

I stopped and turned. "Yes."

"How do you do, old boy?" said a thin, dark-haired chap. "I'm Captain Peters."

"How do you do?" I nodded, shaking the captain by the hand.

"I just wanted to check that General Allcock's instructions were…*clear*," he said.

"Well, I gathered that my platoon is required to bolster the numbers in Dinant until more reinforcements can get there?"

"Yes, and he told you where you'd find the guns?"

"Guns, old boy?" I shrugged. "I don't think that the general mentioned anything specific about guns; other than warning me not to try and fire any of my chaps out of a cannon."

"Uh!" He tutted. "I knew that he'd forget! There are some 25-pounders which he wants you to take with you and deliver to Major Boothroyd."

"Oh, right, okay then," I said. "No problem."

"Splendid." Peters smiled. "And, erm, did the general give you a shilling, at all?"

"Why, yes." I nodded. "Yes, he did."

"Do you suppose that I might have it back?"

"Yes, all right." I shrugged, rummaging in my pocket.

"It's just that he takes handfuls of them from the petty cash without signing for them, you see."

"Oh."

"Mm. He gives them to all-and-sundry, for anything from 'conspicuous pleasantry' to 'outstanding heavy bleeding'."

I pulled out a shilling and handed it to Captain Peters. "Well done, soldier; that's a very affable demeanour you've got there." I winked. "Here, slip this into your little pocket and off you toddle, you young scamp!"

The captain laughed out loud. "Don't," he said, shaking his head. "I get it seven days a week!"

"How *does* he maintain an effective command?" I asked in a lowered voice.

"With round-the-clock supervision and a great deal of assistance," the captain sighed.

Peters thanked me and pointed out the three spanking-new 25-pounders which awaited transportation before trotting off again. (Presumably to continue wet nursing the maladjusted general.)

"All right, gather around, chaps!" I told the lads. "I have received our orders."

"You heard the captain!" Harris barked. "Get your carcasses over 'ere!"

"Thank you, Sergeant." I nodded. "Now then, our fighting prowess is required in Dinant, down in the Ardennes. A bunch of chaps down there need our assistance to hold-back the Hun until more reinforcements arrive, in a day or two. We have also been charged with the task of towing some 25-pounders down there with us. I'm not sure how well the trucks are going to cope with those hills, given all the extra weight, but there we are."

"Hills?" Manning frowned. "I thought that Belgium was all flat, sir."

"Not-so in the south," I told him. "The Ardennes is actually the weathered remains of an ancient mountain range and is typified by steep-sided river valleys and thick forests. Though ordinarily regarded as being two distinct regions, the Ardennes and the Eifel range, in Germany, are actually part of the same geological formation."

"Well," said Manning. "I never knew that!"

"You do now." I winked.

"What you were saying earlier, sir," said Miggs, "about the Great War an' that, is that *we* got dragged into it 'cos of Belgium?"

"Yep." I nodded. "Again, it was down to tiresome treaty obligations and suchlike."

"Bloody Belgium!" he sneered.

"That puts me in mind of the story of an old Belgie priest, of the time," I grinned, "Who looked-up '*Fahk*', phonetically, in his little English dictionary and found, to his surprise, that the word *fake* means 'false' or 'unreal'. He could not, for the life of him, understand why British soldiers should refer to them in this way but, everywhere that he went, he heard them saying 'Fake Belgium' and 'Fake Belgies'."

(The lads had a good old chuckle at that one!)

"Blimey, these are brand, spankin' new," Harris observed, casting his eye over the guns. "None of 'em look like they've ever been fired."

"Detail six men to hitch them up, Sergeant," I told him.

"Yes, sir," he replied. "Miggs, Davenport, Warwick, Tucker, Ferguson and Hawkins; two men to a gun, let's get 'em hitched-up – jaldi!"

"What are you smirking at, Corporal?" I asked Manning as he stood there grinning inanely.

"Fake Belgium, sir." He laughed.

"Young Hinckley didn't seem to find it terribly amusing," I said. "Do you think it went over the top of his head again?"

"Oh no, I think he got it, sir," Manning replied. "But he's still tryin' to work out why that girl was called Nicholas."

"Oh, my God." I chuckled. "I hope somebody's going to enlighten him soon?"

"Nah, sir. The lads are takin' bets on 'ow long it'll be before the penny drops."

"Could be never."

By the time that the ammo had been loaded, all three of the trucks were heaving under the weight.

"Bloody hell; they're almost bottoming-out!" I frowned. "We'd better take it nice and easy."

Wallonia

We set forth again and trundled eastwards across Belgium – through Mons and Charleroi – to Namur, then turned south and followed the narrow, winding road as it meandered up the Meuse valley, through the hills of Wépion and Profondeville.

About half-way between Profondeville and Anhée, however, I noticed that Nelly's fuel gauge was looking a little low and so I signalled the convoy to halt.

"Petrol top-up is it, sir?" said Harris, alighting from Gertie's cab.

"Yep." I nodded. "Three men – Miggs, Davenport and Perkins – get a jerry can each."

Sergeant Harris and I carried-out a quick visual inspection of the vehicles and I was stunned when we came to Bertha, at the rear.

"Manning!" I barked, directing his attention to the empty space behind Bertha. "Where the hell is your gun?"

"Oh no!" he gasped. "Where is it?"

"I asked first!" I glared.

"Oh God, I've lost it!"

"Well, I suggest that you go and bloody-well find it then, lad!" I snapped. "PDQ!"

"Yes, sir." He nodded.

"I don't think Manning's really to blame actually, sir," said Harris. "Look; the bleedin' tow bar's snapped off!"

"Good God!" I seethed; giving Bertha's left rear tyre a kick. "These bloody things are falling apart!"

"I think I see it, sir," said Manning, peering through a pair of field glasses. "It's only about a hundred yards back but it's gone off the road and down into a gulley."

"Right, let's get back there and get a winch cable on it then."

"We, erm, don't have one, sir," said Harris.

"What?"

"None of the vehicles has a winch, sir."

"Uh!" I tutted. "It just keeps on getting better! Okay, ropes it is then."

The runaway 25-pounder had left a scar in its wake which snaked down the side of the valley, through ferns and brambles and pine saplings, to where the stranded artillery piece lay wedged at the top of a deep gulley. Having assessed the situation, I determined that the side of the valley was steep, wet, and slippery enough to necessitate an abseil. "Right, Fidget," I said. "Get down there and attach the tow rope."

"Me, sir?" Ferguson quailed. "Abseil, sir? Down there?"

"Yes, *you*, lad. Off you go!"

"But, sir…"

"Damn it all!" I glared. "Will you just do it?"

(Harris then reminded me that it was Ferguson who, whilst attempting an abseil during training, had plummeted to the deck, breaking several ribs and puncturing a lung.) "Perhaps I'd better do it anyway, sir?" he suggested. "We want to make sure the rope is attached properly, don't we?"

"Mmmm. There is that, I suppose." I nodded. "All right then, Fidget – since you're still on jankers – you'll find an old toothbrush in the toolbox; whilst we extricate the gun, you can go and scrub Gertrude's tyres. I want to see them clean and black and shining before we get them all muddy again!"

"Yes, sir," Ferguson sighed.

I climbed back into Nelly's cab and Harris took the end of the tow rope around a tree, on the opposite side of the road, and abseiled down to the 25-pounder. He tied the rope to the gun's towing point and signalled that it was secure so I began to creep forward and take-up the slack. Inch-by-inch, the gun was slowly hoisted back up to the road, where the lads manhandled it into position. The BL 25-pounder no longer looked all shiny and brand-spanking new.

"Ooh, it's a bit wobbly an' all, sir." Manning frowned. "I think the axle's bent."

"Bloody hell!" I tutted. "Let's get it cleaned-up and have a proper look."

"May I whisper in your ear, sir?" Harris asked quietly.

"Yes, of course, Sa'nt." I nodded. "What's up?"

"I need to requisition some clean pants, sir," he said. "The effort of the abseil... I've still got a bit o' gippy-tum."

"Phew!" I frowned, catching a whiff of him. "Mm, yes, absolutely; go and help yourself...right away."

"Thank you, sir."

"Fidget!" I barked. "Get your worthless backside over here and clean-up this gun, lad!"

"Yes, sir," he grovelled.

Once the gun (and Harris) were cleaned-up, the sergeant and I gave it a proper, thorough, inspection.

"Christ, it *is* wobbly, isn't it?" I frowned. "Oh well, let's get it lashed onto the truck; we'll just have to take it *really* easy the rest of the way."

From somewhere far away to the east came a deep, rumbling noise. "Sounds like thunder, sir," said Warwick. "D'ya think we're in for some more rain?"

"No." I frowned, cocking my head to one side and listening to the distant thudding. "That's not thunder, lad."

We finally arrived in Dinant at 19:20 and a sentry, at the vehicle checkpoint, directed us to Major Boothroyd's command HQ. Dinant was every bit as ghastly and shabby as the rest of bloody Belgium; just smaller. The scenery, of course, was reasonably aesthetically inoffensive; even pleasant. It was, however, full of unwashed, uncouth, and culturally challenged Frogs and Belgies.

We pulled-up at the command centre and I alighted from Nelly's cab. Major Boothroyd took no tracking-down as he was standing nearby giving a petrified-looking young private a severe (and excessively loud) dressing-down. I waited until the ranting major seemed to have run out of rant and then approached him with a salute.

"Major Boothroyd, sir?" I smiled. "I'm Captain Poncenby, sir. We're the First Halb…"

"You're too late!" Boothroyd scowled. "The war's over; you might as well go back home!"

"Sir?"

"I abhor tardiness, Pompendy!"

"Poncenby, sir."

The major looked disdainfully at the trucks. "Oh." He frowned. "Is this it?"

"Yes, sir," I replied. "This is very much *it*."

"Oh dear," he sighed. "Well, unhitch the guns, get the shells unloaded, and then go and park those dreadful things out of the way somewhere; they really are the most frightful eyesore."

"Well, sir," I said. "Needs must, where the Devil…"

"Go and move the damned things then!" he barked.

(Were it not for Boothroyd's rank, I would have pummelled the graceless penis into the middle of 1941!) I left the 25-pounders exactly where they stood and had the lads stack the ammo crates nearby. We then went and parked Nelly, Gertrude and Bertha in a street around the corner.

"Distribute the gin ration, I think, Sergeant," I told Harris.

"Yes, sir."

The 'hurrahs' were markedly less hearty than they had been up until then.

"What about Ferguson, sir?" Harris asked quietly.

"No," I replied. "He's on loss-of-gin for the rest of the day."

"I know, sir," he said, "but look at him."

Ferguson *did* appear to be descending into a bit of a state but I was unmoved. "It wouldn't be good for discipline if I started going-back on my word," I told Harris. "I don't think that the lads would respect me for it."

"Right-ho, sir." He nodded.

Sergeant Harris doled-out the gin and the conversation turned again to our surroundings and the extensive history of warring on the continent.

"European powers have made a battleground of this region for centuries, on account of its strategic importance," I told the chaps. "That big rock, by the river there, is named 'Bayard' after a magical bay horse, in the Old French chanson de geste *Quatre Fils Aymon*, who is said to have leapt from the top of it, whilst fleeing the emperor Charlemagne, and landed right over there on the west bank of the Meuse."

"Blimey!" Harris chuckled. "I'd 'ave a couple o' bob on *him*, in the National!"

"Yeah, not 'alf!" Miggs agreed.

"Charlemagne, sir?" Manning frowned. "Who was he then? I've 'eard of 'im."

"He was king of the Franks, from 768 AD," I told him. "Son of Pepin the Short. The pope made him emperor of the Holy Roman Empire in the year 800 and, by the time that the Saxons came under his control in 804, he ruled over most of Western Europe."

"Oh yeah." Manning nodded. "I thought so."

"In the *Chanson de Roland*, sung by the old twelfth-century troubadours." I went on, "Charlemagne suffers a nightmare, on the eve of the Battle of Roncevaux Pass. The nightmare is set in the Ardennes' forest, where some of his most important battles were fought."

"Cor, it's steeped in history around 'ere then eh, sir?" said Warwick.

"Oh yes," I replied. "Of course, the terrain makes it highly unsuitable for modern, large-scale, military operations but that didn't prevent the Boche from making rapid passage through here during the Battle of the Ardennes in the last war."

"Ri-ight." Hawkins nodded.

"You've no idea what I've just been waffling-on about, do you?" I asked him.

"Not really, sir." He shrugged. "Summink about some bloke called Charlie Maine and a magic, flyin' horse."

"*Charlie Maine*?" I chuckled. "Oh, Hawk-eye, you're priceless, my lad!"

"Thank you very much, sir." He beamed. (The bloody half-wit!)

"How come you know so much about all that history and stuff, sir?" asked Manning.

"Well, I've been expelled from some very good schools," I replied.

"Expelled, sir?" He chuckled. "*You*?"

"Oh, yes. In my adolescence I was, er, a bit of cad, I'm afraid."

"What, you mean you used to skip Latin lessons to go and smoke behind the bike shed?" he scoffed.

"Oh, no, I was a *bona fide* reprobate." I frowned. "I lost count of the number of birchings which I received for my various misdemeanours. It was the army, of course, that finally turned-me-around and made me the man that I am."

"Captain Pondistry?" A voice called out. "Is there a Captain Pondistry here?"

"Sa'ant Harris, do you hear somebody calling my name?" I asked.

Harris cocked his head to one side and listened.

("Captain Ponterbury, perhaps?")

"No, sir." He shrugged. "I've not heard anybody call *your* name, sir."

("Is there a Captain Possibly...possibly?")

"I suppose that I'd better see what it is." I sighed. "It could be something important, after all."

"I'll wager it's about that 25-pounder," said Harris.

"Oh God, yes." I tutted. (The damaged gun had momentarily slipped my mind.) "There's a Captain *Poncenby*, here!" I shouted. "Will *he* do?"

The same young private who had just been on the wrong end of Boothroyd's reprimand came trotting around the corner. "Sorry, Captain Poncenby, sir," he panted. "I don't think that Major Boothroyd caught your name properly."

"No, that's because he couldn't be bothered to listen," I told him.

"I'm afraid that the major wants to speak to you, sir."

"Oh joy!" I exclaimed. "I bet he didn't tell you what it's about either, did he?"

"No, sorry, sir. He just told me to come and find you, sir."

"So, what fetched you such a rollicking just now then, soldier?" I asked the lad, as I strolled next to him.

"Oh, I didn't put enough sugar in the major's tea, sir," he replied.

"Ha-ha!" I chuckled. "No, really though."

"Seriously, sir," he sighed. "Major Boothroyd likes to 'ave three sugars in his char."

"Ugh! You can't taste the tea, surely! What'll he do when supplies run low?"

"Already crossed that bridge, sir – he's rationed the rest of us."

"But that's appalling!" I frowned.

"It's not so bad, sir. One can normally trade something with the chaps who don't take sugar."

"That's hardly the point though, is it, eh?"

Boothroyd and a couple of his lackeys were eyeing-up the guns. "You there, Ponderly!" He scowled.

"Poncenby, sir," I reminded him.

"This weapon's carriage is defective!"

"Hm." I nodded. "My corporal reported that it felt a little unstable when we set-off from Valenciennes."

"Well, what is the point of bringing me wobbly guns?"

"I'm really just the delivery boy, sir." I shrugged. "General Allcock asked that you speak to him directly, should any issue arise, and he'll deal with it personally."

"I shall be doing that forthwith!" Boothroyd scowled.

(*The best of bloody luck to you with that then!*) I chuckled to myself.

The long and the short of it was that we were required to march eastwards and rendezvous with a certain Captain Farringdon, on the outskirts of a neighbouring village called Trouvière.

"Tonight's password is *Boiled beef and carrots*," said Boothroyd. "Now, you won't forget that, will you?"

"Golly," I sighed. "I shall *try* not to, sir."

Boothroyd shot me a seething glare but said nothing else.

The road into Trouviére was little more than a narrow track, lined with tall evergreen trees, hawthorns, brambles and tufts of long, coarse grasses. Somewhat dolefully, the platoon marched down the lane and we soon came to another checkpoint with a sentry box.

"Halt! Who goes there?" a voice demanded. "Friend or foe?"

"What a damn fool question!" I exclaimed. "Who the hell is going to say 'foe'?"

"Eh?"

"What if I said that I was Heinrich bloody Himmler? What then, eh?"

"You're not, are you?"

"Well now, what do *you* think?"

"Erm…well, what's the password?"

"Boiled-beef and carrots," I sighed impatiently.

"Is that right?" the sentry asked, turning aside.

"Dunno," another voice replied. "What day is it?"

"What day is it?" the first sentry called out.

"It's Thursday." I tutted. (*'For God's sake!'*)

There followed a brief pause, during which the flipping of pages could be heard. "Yeah, that's right," the second voice said eventually. "Thursday: Bottled beef and carrots."

"*Bottled* beef?" quizzed the first.

"That's what is says 'ere."

"Oh, stop wasting my time, you bloody idiots!" I said, marching onwards. "Hawk-eye, I think I've found a couple of new chums for you!"

It must once have been a picturesque little rural Belgie village, Trouviére. All that remained now, though, was the occasional gate post, or the corner of a building, poking defiantly through the mass of blasted rubble and debris and dirt – all that was left of some poor sod's home and possessions. Everywhere that one looked, were tiny reminders of a constant factor in all such conflicts; the ordinary people who get caught in the bloody middle.

"Captain Farringdon?" I smiled. "I'm Poncenby, old boy; we're the 1st Halberds."

"Oh," the captain sighed, his shoulders sagging.

"Well, *you* needn't sound so pleased to see us as well!" I frowned.

"Sorry, old chap," said Farringdon. "But we were expecting rather more *substantial* reinforcements."

"General Allcock *did* say that he has a company on its way," I told him, "but they may not be here for a day or two, I'm afraid."

"I don't know that there will be anyone left by then."

"It's *that* bad then?"

"Mm." He frowned. "If Jerry knew how thin-on-the-ground we are now... There are plenty of empty dugouts anyway."

"All right, chaps, find yourselves dugouts and get your bunks made up," I told the lads.

The dugouts were cramped, dank, and stinking; each was about ten feet square, shored-up with bare timbers and sandbags, and had a roof of corrugated iron with a protective covering of about two feet of earth.

"Oh God, what poo-hole!" Manning groaned, peering inside one of the dingy structures.

"Nonsense," I told him. "Why, this is positively palatial; and *such* an exclusive neighbourhood too."

"It's a bloody toilet, sir!" he sneered.

"Perhaps you'd prefer a little shell-scrape, out there in the middle of no man's land?"

"No, sir," he said flatly. "It's a, erm...yeah, it's a nice little place actually – I like the roof in particular."

"Ha-ha-ha!" I chuckled. "Welcome to the Hotel Trouviére! Make yourselves at home, chaps; you'll soon get used to the stink. The neighbours down the road are a bit of a frightful bunch, but we're going to be killing them soon anyway!"

I left the chaps to get settled-in and liaised with Captain Farringdon, who was standing in the firing trench, outside his dugout, scanning the battlefield through a periscope.

"All quiet, old chap?" I asked.

"What-ho, Poncenby!" He smiled. "Yes, all quiet – for now. Just keeping an eye out for one of my lieutenant's patrols actually."

"Ah." I nodded, as I followed him inside.

"So, you've met Sheridan then?" he asked.

"Sheridan?" I shrugged.

"Sorry, old boy, that's Boothroyd."

"Oh, *him*." I frowned. "Yes, we crossed paths."

"Cross swords too?"

"Hmmm. Rather."

"Yes, he has that effect on people." The captain sighed. "He's, erm…"

"A penis?" I suggested.

"Ha-ha-ha!" Farringdon chuckled. "I couldn't have put it better myself, old chap!"

The captain's laughter drew many staring eyes and it became apparent that humour had largely deserted the chaps at the front. This was not remotely surprising, of course; most of the poor blighters looked like they'd had a damned rough time of it.

"Tell you what," I said, rummaging inside my tunic. "I was given this." (I handed Captain Farringdon the bottle of rum.) "Why don't you and your lads have it, eh?"

"Eurgh; no fear!" he gasped. "That stuff turns you queer!"

I stared at him for a silent moment before we both guffawed loudly, drawing more quizzical looks.

"Good man!" I chuckled.

"Thanks awfully, old boy." Farringdon smiled. He filled his hip flask, poured a measure into his tin mug, and then handed the bottle to his sergeant, who went to distribute the rest amongst his men. (A few subdued 'hurrahs' could be heard nearby.)

"So, what's the score out there?" I asked, nodding towards no man's land.

The captain's countenance transformed into a deep frown; "It's been pretty disastrous of late, frankly," he sighed.

"Well, I'm sorry to hear that," I told him. "But don't call me *Frankly*, eh?"

"Hm?"

"Hugo'll do." I winked.

"Oh! Ha-ha-ha!" Farringdon chortled. "I'm Charles, old boy."

"Glad to know you." I nodded, shaking him by the hand.

Farringdon then elucidated on the current situation and the picture which he painted was rather grim. "Sometimes the artillery bombardment is bloody *unbelievable*!" He frowned. "And then, of course, comes the infantry charge; the machine guns and mortars."

I nodded slowly. "Hmmm."

"Well, all of that is one thing," he went on, "but there's a damned panzer detachment that keeps on popping-up out of nowhere and blasting everything in sight to bloody bits."

"Right, well, my orders were simple," I told him. "My chaps are to assist in holding this line, by whatever means necessary, until reinforcements arrive. All that we need to do now is work out just what means *is* necessary."

"Ooh!" Farringdon suddenly winced. "Bugger!"

"All right?" I enquired, mildly concerned. "Are you wounded, old boy?"

Farringdon shook his head. "Piles." He scowled.

"Haemorrhoids? Golly, are they, erm…*external*?"

"Very." He nodded. "Like a bunch of pendulous bloody grapes!"

"Ooh!" I grimaced, sucking air in between my teeth. "No Prep. H?"

"Ran out weeks ago," he replied, shaking his head forlornly.

"Well, listen," I said, "I don't know how effective it is, but I've seen plantains growing around here; scrunch-up some leaves and apply the juice two or three times a day."

"Really?" He frowned. "Plantain leaves?"

"Mm." I nodded. "Or an infusion of leaves and flowers from camomile. The bark of oak or elm, made into a decoction, is supposed to work too."

"How remarkable!" Farringdon exclaimed. "Well, I shall bloody-well try that. Thanks awfully."

"Not at all." I winked. "I'd be interested to know how effective you find it actually."

I left Farringdon's dugout, returned to the platoon, and had Sergeant Harris issue the bedtime gin.

"Ferguson," I said. "Though it has not yet turned midnight, I have decided to include you in this gin ration."

"Oh, f-fank you, sir," he stammered. "You're such a good sport, sir!"

"Get it down you, lad," I told him. "And just be more careful where you point that odious backside of yours in future, eh?"

"Yes, sir." He frowned. "Sorry, sir."

After the gin ration, I instructed Harris to ready the men for an inspection of their feet.

"Foot inspection!" he bawled. "Let's see 'em; 'ave 'em out! They'd better be clean, dry, and lightly powdered – or else!"

I worked my way along the line examining soles, heels and toes.

"Not too bad." I nodded. "That verruca looks to be clearing-up, Miggs."

"Yeah, I reckon it'll soon be gone now, sir," he replied.

"As you know, I usually advise against bursting blisters," I told Warwick. "But you can pop that one, if it becomes too painful."

"Right-ho, sir," said Warwick. "It's not givin' me any gip at the mo."

Eventually I came to the low-brow and obtuse paradigm of arrested development that was Private Hawkins. "Ugh!" I grimaced. "Hawkins, get those bloody talons of yours clipped at once!"

"Talents, sir?" He frowned gormlessly.

"*Talons*, lad!" I tutted. "Cut those horrible yellow nails!"

"Oh." He nodded. "Yes, sir."

The lads then slipped their feet back into their boots and shuffled-off, into their respective dugouts, to bed-down for the night.

"How are you feeling about the task in hand then?" I asked Harris.

"In truth, sir," he said. "I can't wait to get stuck into the rotten blighters!"

"That's the spirit." I winked. "Good night, Sergeant."

"G'night, sir." He nodded.

The Battle of Trouviére

I find myself hard-pressed to even attempt to describe the events of the following day; pages of evocative adjectives could not begin to adequately convey even the vaguest impression of the awful reality of it. In all honesty, I would be more comfortable having to write about Scandinavian fish-preserving practises in thirteenth-century Norway whilst rabid, syphilitic Valkyries flayed me with bramble canes and stinging nettles. (In fact, I'd just as soon be severely beaten about the head and neck with a red-hot poker but there we are!)

A loud whooshing noise was followed by an ear-splitting and seismic explosion; clods of earth, shards of splintered timber and chunks of raw, red meat were scattered everywhere as Jerry's big guns opened-up and 128 mm shells began to rain down. So intense and relentless was the artillery pounding that it quickly broke the mind, spirit and bowel-control of the less stout-hearted. The scene was quite unlike anything which I had ever witnessed before and no amount of training or drilling could ever possibly prepare one for the abject horror of such unbelievable carnage, devastation and wholesale slaughter. For hour-after-hour, the brutal bombardment continued; until one was forced to conclude that this must, surely, be the very end of the world! (As one may imagine, for many hundreds of hapless souls, it *was*.)

I'd seen chaps killed before, of course; Tuppy Horton was the first; accidentally garrotted by his own braces, whilst playing 'Cowboys and Indians' back in 1922. There had been raw terror in poor old Tuppy's bulging, bloodshot eyes as he dangled by his neck from that apple tree, while the rest of us just stood and gawped.

Then there was Stiffy Plantaganet, who was knocked down on the tennis courts at his home, by a motor car driven (in reverse) by his inebriated Aunt Agatha. I seem to remember that Plantaganet was absent from school for quite some time before it was announced by the Headmaster that old Stiffy had finally shuffled-off his bucket, kicked his clogs, and popped his mortal coil.

I have just remembered another one, too: Benjamin Alistair Drayton, who drowned in Tatlock Pond, (Whilst I warmed my palms, on his sister Millicent's bare breasts, in a nearby thicket). I didn't see him drown, of course (having, as I did, my hands rather full at the time), but I watched Mr Mulgrew and Constable Pinchworthy fish Drayton's lifeless, floppy corpse from the stagnant water afterwards.

This was the first time that I'd seen a chap killed *so* horribly though; a shell had exploded nearby and shrapnel had completely smashed Simpson's face in; his belly was torn wide-open and his wet, shiny innards spilled out onto the brown earth. (Needless to say, he did not live for long.) I paused for a moment, drew a deep breath, and then vomited; so hard that my backside trumpeted loudly. ("Pffrrrt!")

The heavy artillery bombardment subsided and, before long, the Jerry infantry and armour were moving-up and we came under fire from Panzers and MG34 machine guns. Rifle shots rang-out in answer, from up and down our lines, and were soon joined by the rattle of Lewis and Bren guns. Deep, booming thuds added to the din as our mortar crews sent their three-inch rounds arcing high overhead and off into the middle-distance.

"Should we wait until we see the whites of their eyes, Sarge?" asked Miggs.

"Don't be so bloody stupid, lad!" Harris barked. "If Jerry's in range, you sodding-well shoot 'im!"

"I got one, sir!" Davenport declared jubilantly. (I yanked him down into the trench, by his webbing, just as two 7.62 mm rounds dinged off his steel helmet.)

"Well done, Private Tricky," I told him. "But keep that noggin down or Jerry *will* reciprocate!"

"Yes, sir," he spluttered, wide-eyed with adrenaline.

Suddenly, a young blonde lad; in strange, grey fatigues; tumbled into our trench, clutching a bloody Jerry Gewehr rifle, with a fixed bayonet. Without hesitation, or any conscious act of will, I gave him three rounds from my revolver; two in the chest and one in the head.

"Pffrrrt!" went Jerry's rotten arse, as his bowels evacuated, and the already whiffy trench suddenly filled with a stink like that of rotting cabbage!

"Heurp!" I retched.

"Gas!" Hawk-eye gasped.

"No, it's not!" I yelled. "Not *that* sort, anyway." (I showed him the nasty Nazi mess in the corner.)

"Eurgh!" he retched. "Bloody 'ell!"

"Miggs! Tubby! Get that machine gunner!" I cried. "Forty yards, half-right, in the bush!"

"I see him, sir!" Miggs declared and they both directed their fire as ordered.

Bugger me if, right at that moment, another sausage-eating bounder didn't come blundering right into our bloody trench! For a moment, Hawkins just stood there gawping at the Jerry spread-eagled at his feet.

"Bayonet, Hawk-eye!" I bellowed, gesticulating wildly.

As though the words had activated some hitherto dormant part of Hawk-eye's little mind, he suddenly sprang into action. "Aargh!" he screeched, thrusting the full length of his bayonet into the enemy again and again.

"Good lad!" I told him.

"Eurgh! He fuckin' stinks!" Hawkins retched. (He then vomited all-over the dead Jerry.)

"Eyes-front, lad!" I chuckled. "There's plenty more where that rotten bastard came from!"

"That bugger's got a flamethrower, sir!" Harris exclaimed. "A hundred yards, quarter-left, by the oak tree."

"Yep, seen!" I nodded. "Manning! One hundred yards, one quarter left, oak tree; I do *not* want that bounder getting within fifty yards of our bloody line!"

"I see 'im, sir!" Manning replied. (He turned his Bren gun on the flame-thrower-wielding swine and must've hit Jerry's fuel tank because the cad went-up with a satisfying BOOM!) "Have *that* you bastard!" Manning cried.

"Well done, lad!" I beamed. "Eyes-front now!"

The long day went on and on, in similar fashion, until eventually (and only then because the evening drew-in and the light became poor) the fighting began to subside and, one by one, the guns finally quieted.

Everywhere that one looked; the ground was scorched, cratered, and littered with shards of metal and pieces of burnt wood, fabric and raw flesh. The air was thick with the most noxious stench of acrid smoke, blood, vomit, scattered intestines and faecal material. From every direction came harrowing cries of human suffering; ranging from distant, shrill screams; through agonised groaning and impassioned pleas for help (or death); to the nearby wheezing and gurgling of the soon-to-be deceased.

Damage reports and casualty assessments started to come in and the figures made for rather grim reading. I gazed in wonder at the staggering (and still growing) number of men already killed or incapacitated during the course of that one day's engagement.

As soon as the opportunity arose, I made a tour of the camp to lend an ear to the many, many disgruntled gripes of the rank-and-file soldiery. "All right there, Manning?" I winked as I returned his salute. "Good to see you in one piece, lad."

"You'll 'ave t' speak up, sir," he said. "I can't hear a bloody thing!"

I signed to him, and mouthed my words very carefully so that he could read my lips. "Good to see you!"

"Oh, yeah." He nodded. "You too, sir!"

Manning's face – now grubby and blood-spattered – looked ten years older than it had done that morning and there was swelling and purple bruising around his right eye. All down his front were burgundy-coloured handprints; as though some poor beggar had been gripping his tunic during their death-throes (which, it turned out, they *had*).

"Hell of a day, wasn't it?" I frowned.

"I ain't never known nothin' like it in me bloody life, sir!" Manning spluttered. "I shat m'self, sir! Actually, just…*shat* myself!"

"Well," I said, "I doubt that you're alone there, lad – far from it. How did you get the shiner?"

"I copped Sanderson's 'ead in the face, sir."

"That was unfortunate."

"Yeah, it was, sir – the rest of his mangled self was thirty bloody yards away!"

"Hmmm," I sighed. "Hell of a battle!"

"It was a bloody massacre from what I saw, sir!"

Losses amongst our platoon had been mercifully few but there were, unsurprisingly, no 'hurrahs' when Sergeant Harris doled out the early evening gin ration.

The Tank Hunters

I liaised with Captain Farringdon to discuss how the Hun's efforts could best be thwarted. "Well, their big artillery pieces, over there in Ciney and Rochefort, are well-beyond our reach, of course," he said. "It's those bloody tanks that *really* give me the willies anyway; some of them have three thirty-cal machine guns, in addition to the main weapon, and they're *so* mobile."

"But how the hell is Jerry getting them through?"

"The only conceivable way is down this road, the Rue de Ciney, to the east," said Farringdon. "The hills and the marshy ground, to the north and south of the road, present a bit of an obstacle to armoured vehicles. I have a patrol out tonight, thickening-up the natural defences with some mines."

"Jolly good show." I nodded. (As Farringdon and I continued to study maps and patrol reports, a daft notion kept trying to elbow its way into my mind.) "This little stretch of road, through the gorge here, would be a *great* location for an ambush," I mused. "The lead vehicle will be right on the crest of this little ridge, with his gun pointing in the air and his belly exposed. We need only to disable it – blow one of its tracks off or something – and the entire column will come grinding to a halt."

"I say they'd be sitting ducks!"

"Absolutely." I nodded. "Have some chaps with AT weapons, concealed in these defilade positions, and we can then attack, enfilade, for maximum effect. We then pull-back to here and let the big guns annihilate whatever is left."

"I like it, old boy!" Farringdon declared. "I like it *very* much."

"All of that wreckage will make a splendid roadblock against further incursions too."

"I'm afraid that there's precious little in the way of infantry AT weaponry about."

"I've got a couple of .55 Boys rifles," I told him, "and my chaps can knock-up a few improvised incendiaries. That and few grenades and mortars ought to suffice."

"Good Lord, are you sure?"

"Oh, yes. Those bloody panzers aren't as invulnerable as they might seem. Besides, all we need to do is to disable them and the artillery can finish 'em off."

"Well, that's the trap, then," said the captain. "With what are we to bait it though? Jerry must be well-aware of the hazards."

"I wonder if, perhaps, the Hun needs a little *push* rather than a pull."

"Not sure that I follow you, old boy."

"I'd like to somehow bloody the Hun's nose and see if we can goad him into a hasty response."

"Golly, I think that I might know how," said Farringdon. "It'd be bloody dicey but…"

"Mm? Tell me more."

One of Farringon's standing patrols had apparently spotted a detachment of half a dozen panzers, refuelling in a side road off the Rue de Ciney, the night before. "I've just been told that they used the same location again tonight," he said.

"So," I mused, my eyes narrowing, "they'll probably be there tomorrow night as well, eh?"

"Mm. I'd say that it was highly likely."

"Well, it's a nice, secluded, little spot to refuel in, but it'd be hell to escape from if caught unawares and attacked. Can we *get* to it though?"

"I think so." He nodded. "We've found quite a sizeable gap in the line, between these two divisions."

"Plenty of places along that stretch where a few quiet chaps could slip behind the lines and back again, eh?"

"There's a good half a mile of unguarded open countryside." He nodded. "I just don't have enough chaps left to man these positions *and* carry-out an effective tank-hunting patrol."

"Well, I reckon that I could put together a dozen-strong team from my chaps," I told him. "It'll be painfully slow-going, through the forest at night, but at least we already have a route."

"Perhaps we should iron-out the creases tomorrow then," he yawned. "I'm sure that we could both use some sleep, eh?"

"Yes, indeed." I nodded. "I'll speak to you again in the morning, eh? Goodnight, Charles."

"Goodnight, Hugo, old boy," Farringdon replied, yawning again.

I returned to the chaps and had Sergeant Harris distribute the bedtime gin; but forbade any 'hurrahs'. (Not that the lads were in a particularly 'hurrah' sort of mood anyway, after the day that we'd just had!)

"Did you and Captain Farringdon come up with a plan then, sir?" asked Manning.

"Mm. I think that we *might* have the germ of a little caper," I replied. "Farringdon has patrols out tonight so we shall have a much clearer picture in the morning. Better get some shut eye, eh lads?"

There came a chorus of affirmatives and the chaps started to shuffle-off to their respective dugouts.

"Warwick and Davenport; I've got you two down for first stag," said Harris. "You will not smoke; you will not stand there flapping your lips like a pair of old women; you're probably gonna get cold, and bored too, so no playing silly buggers – all right?"

"Yes, sir." They both nodded.

"Good. Off you go then."

The morning brought no heavy artillery bombardment but, throughout the day, sporadic exchanges of small arms and light mortar fire broke-out, up and down the line, as Jerry probed and tested our defences and was met with fierce resistance. I spent a good deal of time studying the landscape through field glasses and then gathered the chaps around me and revealed, with the aid of maps and diagrams, the nature of the proposed operation. "Captain Farringdon and I have conceived of a very cunning and audacious caper," I told them. "I shall be leading a dozen-strong team on a tank-hunting patrol this very evening."

"Tank-hunting, sir?" Miggs frowned. "Blimey, that sounds *frightfully* dangerous!"

"It's not without danger, of course." I shrugged. "But, once we know exactly what we're dealing with, we also know *how* to deal with it."

"Mm?"

"The *PanzerKampfwagen III* – or Mk III Panzer – weighs approximately twenty-three tons and has frontal armour plating which is nearly three inches thick," I said, prodding at a crude sketch. "Its principal weapon is a thirty-seven-millimetre gun – which is about an inch and a half, to you and I – and most are also equipped with two, or three, thirty-cal machine guns."

"Bloody hell!" Warwick gasped.

"Yes; formidable." I nodded. "No tank, however, is entirely invulnerable to attack; even from lowly infantry: the tracks are an obvious weak point and, in its less well-protected spots, the thickness of the Panzer's armour is only three sixteenths of an inch; its speed, off-road, is limited to about twelve miles-an-hour; the principal weapon can aim no closer than about twenty yards away and visibility from inside is so awful that, if you're within about ten yards, the crew won't even be able to see you."

"Now, that *is* startin' to sound a little bit less daunting, sir," said Miggs.

"Precisely." I smiled. "Goliath was slain by the lowliest of shepherd boys – and with nothing but a slingshot. So, who wants to volunteer for the operation?" (There was a pitiful show of hands.) "Come on now, lads!" I urged. "It's a marvellous opportunity to demonstrate the halberdier's legendary and fearsome fighting abilities!" (Enthusiasm was still found to be wanting.) "There's an extra gin ration for patrol members."

"I'm up for it, sir!" said Miggs.

"Oh, yeah, count *me* in!" Warwick nodded. (There was, thereafter, no shortage of keen petitioners.)

I would sooner have had Harris *and* Manning on the team but, since my sergeant was so well-versed in the art of killing tanks, it would be necessary to leave Corporal Manning commanding the rest of the platoon.

Aside from Harris and Manning, Private 'Tubby' Tucker was the only other of my chaps who was proficient with the stonking-great .55 calibre Boys anti-tank rifle. The monstrous five-foot-two-inch bolt-action 'elephant gun' had a barrel length of three feet and weighed-in at 35 lbs.

"Ooh!" Tubby beamed. "A Boys rifle!"

"Yep. It's a bloody *man's* rifle that!" I winked.

I'd not long returned to my dugout when Captain Farringdon came trotting in looking rather anxious.

"Hugo, I'm afraid that Sheridan wasn't very impressed with our little scheme." He frowned. "I've just been informed that he's on his way over here."

"Oh, bloody hell," I sighed. "I need *that* like a ruddy bayonet up the jacksy."

The major turned-up shortly thereafter. "Right, now, what's all this nonsense about a covert tank-hunting patrol?" he sneered.

"Well, sir," said Farringdon. "We've come-up with…"

"Oh, shut up, Farringdon!" Boothroyd snapped. "Every time that you open your mouth, a great load of frightful verbal diarrhoea comes pouring out of it!" (Farringdon shrugged and embarked upon a thorough inspection of the ceiling.) "You, Pongetry!" he barked, pointing at me with his baton. "Explain yourself!"

I joined Farringdon in his examination of the corrugated tin roof.

"Well?"

"Oh, I'm afraid that Pongetry was killed, sir," I said.

Boothroyd screwed-up his nose. "What?"

"Captain Pongetry, sir; he was shredded to bits by MG34s, you know. I'm his replacement; *Pon-cen-by*," (I noticed the corners of Captain Farringdon's eyes crease; his jaw clamped tight and his bottom lip began to quiver.)

"Are you trying to be funny, Captain?" The major glared.

"No, sir," I replied, "there was no effort whatsoever to that end."

Boothroyd narrowed his eyes. "Well, what's this rubbish about tank-hunting, eh?"

"We have a splendid opportunity to hit-back at the Hun, sir," I told him. "And right where it hurts, too!"

I briefly outlined our plan – pointing-out its many positive aspects – but Major Sheridan 'Penis' Boothroyd was thoroughly unimpressed. "I don't care for your little scheme actually," he sneered. "I want you to assault those observation posts down the road!"

"I don't think that would be at all wise, sir."

"I don't care what you think!" He glowered. "I want those OPs destroyed."

"Sir, those positions are *very* heavily defended; a frontal assault, down that road, would be utter suicide."

"My God! I can't believe what I'm hearing! Stop questioning my orders and go and bloody-well do it!"

"I'm sorry but I can't do that, sir."

"What?" the major roared. "You bloody-well will!"

"No, sir," I said firmly. "I won't."

"I could shoot you for disobeying a direct order, you know!" he yelled, brandishing his revolver.

"Not if it contradicts a prior order issued by a higher-ranking officer, sir," I told him. "My brief from General Allcock..."

"How dare you?" he gasped. "How bloody dare you?"

"... Was to assist in any way which would halt the German advance..."

"I'll see you face a firing squad, you impudent swine!"

"... Until reinforcements arrive. The mass suicide of an entire platoon would not be conducive to achieving that goal...*sir*."

"I'll do it, you know!" he screamed. "I'll shoot you!"

"You'd better shoot all of the witnesses too then, sir," I said calmly. "There's only about four hundred of 'em within earshot."

"My God! You..."

"And then, of course, you'll have to shoot Colonel Brompton and General Allcock, General Gort, Mr Churchill..."

One of Boothroyd's lackeys suddenly interrupted. "Excuse me, Major," said the sergeant. "Sorry, sir, but there's a Colonel Brompton on the telephone; he did say it was rather urgent."

"Wait there!" Boothroyd scowled as he stamped-off outside.

"Bloody hell," Farringdon gasped. "You like to live dangerously don't you, old boy?"

"Him?" I shrugged. "Huh! He knows damned-well that I'm right; I'm not under Sheridan's command; *my* orders came from the general!"

Boothroyd did not return in person but sent word that Colonel Brompton had given our 'hare-brained scheme' the go-ahead.

"Phew!" Farringdon sighed. "Well, Hugo, you needn't bother coming back if you don't pull it off."

"Oh, we'll pull it off all right," I assured him. "My chaps might look like a bloody shower but they're a sterling bunch of lads really," (*Sounded* pretty convincing, didn't it? Hmmm…)

Operation Slingshot

I briefed the patrol on the route we would be following; the positions of friendly and enemy forces in the area; the time scale for the operation; and the passwords and recognition signals which would be in use that night. I then rounded-up all the empty liquor bottles which could be found and carefully filled them with petrol before replacing their caps.

"Aren't you gonna stuff wicks in 'em, sir?" asked Davenport.

"No, there are going to be plenty of sources of ignition in the target area by the time that we deploy these. And, by not lighting them, we shan't give away any more information about our positions than is necessary."

"Ah, that's very good thinking, sir!" He nodded.

"That's what I'm here for." I winked.

I stashed the petrol bombs near the gin palace and we spent the rest of the afternoon planning and practising what we would later be doing, behind the lines, for real. "Each of these rocks is about the same weight as our incendiaries," I told the petrol bomb detail. "Practise throwing them until you're getting them inside the target area *every* time."

As I went to attend to another matter, I suddenly spotted Wonky Warwick, with a bottle to his lips.

"Bleurgh!" he retched, vomiting hard. (His arse erupted too: "Pffrrrt!")

"What the hell are you doing there, Warwick?" I roared. "How dare you drink my petrol?"

"Ugh! I didn't know it was petrol, sir!" he gagged. "Bleurgh!" ("Pffrt!")

"Then, you thought that it was gin to which you were helping yourself, eh?"

"Well, sir," he spluttered. "I erm…it's been *forever* since we last 'ad any, sir."

"No, lad, it's been since 14:20; that's about two hours."

"Oh, God, is that all?"

"I could have you shot for such an attempted misappropriation of the king's liquor, you know."

"You won't though, will you, sir?" he gasped.

"I haven't made my mind up yet," I told him. "But I think that I probably ought to."

"Please don't, sir!"

"Away and tell Sergeant Harris that you're on report; and *why* – he's to put you on jankers and find something to occupy you whilst I consider the matter."

"Please don't shoot me, sir – I'm engaged to be wed!"

"Away!" I glared (whilst I could still keep a straight face).

As the afternoon wore-on, and the sun began to sink towards the horizon, the time for us to embark upon our mission rapidly approached. The first thing to do was to check everybody's kit and make damned sure that everything was secure and that nothing rattled or squeaked. It was still, at that time, a common practise to wear PT shoes (plimsolls), instead of great, clunky artillery boots, for such covert operations.

"Everyone is to go and have a good old clear-out too," I told them. "Whether you feel like it or not. I won't have anyone getting caught-short out there and betraying our position by soiling themselves!"

The patrol, (whom the other chaps nicknamed 'The Deadly Dozen') blacked-up and made its way, through the village, to the last security checkpoint. I gave the sentry the recognition signal and password and we set off, across no man's land, on the most audacious and dangerous escapade in which we had ever been collectively involved. (I must here admit to a very small, but persistent, twitching of the sphincter on my part!)

The first leg of our route took us fifty-seven yards eastwards, on a magnetic bearing of 102°, across the Rue de Houyet, to our first rendezvous point (RV); the bombed-out ruins of a farmhouse. When we reached the roadside, I signalled the patrol to halt and we grouped-up – to keep a look-out all around – before crossing, one at a time, and re-grouping on the other side. After a quick (but thorough) sweep of the ruin, I took a bearing and signalled my intention to move-on to the next RV; a small copse wood, eighty-three yards away, on a bearing of 131°. Cautiously, and in single file, we picked our way across a wide meadow, towards the dark clump of trees.

We had crept forward about sixty yards, when I suddenly smelled cigarette smoke and signalled the patrol to go-to-ground. As we lay there, listening intently and not daring even to breathe, we all heard the tell-tale crack of a twig underfoot. My heart pounded in my ears as a four-man Jerry patrol made its way past us – not ten bloody feet away; and *smoking*, too, if you will! (The faint odour of cigarette smoke, though, was quickly overwhelmed by an altogether more fearsome stink.)

"*Phew! Vas ist das?*" one of the Jerries gasped, sniffing the air.

His chum stopped and sniffed too. "*Ugh! Das ist der hundscheissa, Helmut!*" (That is dog's shit, Helmut!)

One of the stupid buggers then lit a match in order to examine the dog's mess on his footwear!

"*Ugh! Es ist Durchfall!*" he gasped. ("It is diarrhoea!")

"*Eurgh!*" the other one grimaced. "*Es ist gelb; das ist schrecklich!*" ("It's yellow; that is horrible!")

"*Kommen, Helmut! Schnell!*"

"*Ich kommen, Klaus.*"

The dozy Nazi wiped his boot in the grass and then he and his rotten pals buggered off. (The sausage-munching swine were damned lucky that we had bigger fish to fry, that's all!)

Miggs crawled-up, leaned-in close, and whispered in my ear. "Eurgh, I stink, sir!" he said. "That rotten bastard wiped his shitty boot on me!"

I grimaced, shrugged, and turned-away to take another bearing (and breathe some fresher air).

We made our way to the last RV and then took-up our positions, overlooking the objective. It was not long before a low, rumbling noise heralded the approach of our quarry; half a dozen MkIII Panzers pulled-up, in a tight column formation, and their crews began to dismount and set about replenishing the thirsty tanks, utterly unaware of our presence. (And blissfully ignorant, therefore, of what was about to befall them.)

I gave the signal to open fire and all hell broke loose down in the narrow lane. The Boys rifles proved surprisingly effective, when directed at the panzers' thinly armoured rears, and both the lead vehicle and the backmarker were quickly disabled. Engines started-up and panic-stricken drivers tried to scramble from the unfolding nightmare. As the second vehicle in the convoy accelerated forward, a section of its smashed track shot out behind it and decapitated one of his fleeing comrades. Our machine gunners cut-down another eight or ten Jerries as panzer crews abandoned their flaming vehicles and attempted to scarper.

A lovely big fire had broken-out down there so I gave the petrol bombers their signal and they began to lob their incendiaries into the middle of the already blazing scene of carnage and confusion.

I laid-down some covering fire and signalled the patrol to withdraw. (Just for good measure, I lobbed a couple of hand grenades, in the direction of the blazing tanks, before we slipped-away into the night.)

We returned to Trouviére via an entirely different route from the outgoing one (as was standard procedure) and made our way back as quickly as we could; six exploding Panzers would certainly have attracted an awful lot of attention and Jerry might already be hot on our heels. (In the event, though, we managed to steal back into the village undetected by enemy troops.)

Captain Farringdon was ecstatic. "My God!" he exclaimed. "We could see the fire and hear the explosions from here! If *that* hasn't irked them into something hasty, I don't know what will. The chatter, on the wireless, is that they were attacked with hand grenades and bottles of gin!"

"Huh! Do they really think that we'd waste good gin on the likes of *them*?" I chuckled.

"Anyway, all the pieces are now in place." Farringdon smiled. "Anything which tries to come down that road is going to be blasted to bits!"

The squad spent most of the next day, dug-in at the ambush site, waiting patiently.

Such a position begins as a simple slit trench, six feet long, eighteen inches to two feet wide (the narrower, the better), and as deep as the armpits of the tallest man. This two-man 'firing trench' is normally then provided with a protective roof at one end, which is covered with eighteen inches of soil, and incorporating gaps through which grenades can be thrown. The basic firing trench is then extended by five feet, with a similar overhead covering, to form a 'shelter trench' at one end (in which to sleep). A four-man trench is simply twice as long, with a shelter trench at each end. Where possible, turf should be re-laid over the top to aid concealment. (I'd had the foresight, of course, to detail the rest of the platoon to construct three such four-man trenches overnight, whilst we carried-out the main mission.)

"I need a clear-out, sir," said Miggs, as I was scanning the road through field glasses.

"So have one." I shrugged.

Miggsy went outside, dug himself a hole, and whipped his britches down. "PFRRPLLRRRT!" went his arse and the whole trench filled a foul and fetid stink.

"Jesus!" I gasped, my eyes watering.

The awful pong lingered long after Miggs had covered the nasty stuff with soil and filled-in the hole.

"Ooh, that was rotten!" He declared. "Can you smell it?"

We all nodded. "Mm," (It is some small mercy that the human olfactory apparatus quickly tires of an odour and soon becomes pretty insensitive to it.)

Eventually, there was movement, away down the road, and I ordered everybody to stand-to.

"Come and get it, you sausage-eating bastards!" Davenport scowled.

A barrage of artillery, mortars, and machine gun fire preceded the arrival of the armoured units and a wave of infantry began to surge forward. Before long though, the tanks came rumbling down the road towards our meticulously planned and carefully prepared ambush.

BOOM! The lead vehicle was enveloped in a red-orange fireball, as it triggered the AT mine on the road, and a pall of filthy black smoke rose into the air. Back down the line, more panzers started to go up in flames as the grenades, mortars and Molotov's started to fly. The column tried to fan-out and press-on but any which strayed from the road also soon fell victim to more mines.

The tanks being temporarily immobile and in disarray, I gave the signal to withdraw before our 60-pounders' five-inch shells began to rain-down indiscriminately all over the killing ground. We pulled back, and re-joined the main body of troops, ready to engage any infantry who managed to get through.

Before long, all of the filthy Jerries had either been killed or had retreated back down the road, leaving two-dozen 23-ton lumps of smouldering, dead panzer littering the gorge. It was bloody beautiful!

I glanced to my left and noticed that medics were carrying-out frantic chest compressions and mouth-to-mouth on poor old Wonky Warwick, who was covered in blood.

"How's he doing?" I asked.

"I'm sorry, sir," Roberts replied. "We've lost 'im."

"What?"

Trubshaw had claret all up his arms. "There was an arterial bleed, sir," he explained. "By the time I'd managed to find the artery and tie it off he'd gone into shock and..."

"Keep going," I said.

"We'll keep on going for as long as you say, sir, but it'd be to no avail."

"All right then." I sighed, rubbing my forehead. "I suppose that you might as well...stop."

"Time of death; 13:55," said Roberts, scribbling it down in his little pad.

Manning came trotting back from further down the line. "Is he all right, sir?" he asked, nodding towards Warwick. (I shook my head but said nothing.) "I'm afraid we lost Denton and McKilroy, too." He frowned.

"Bloody hell!" I tutted. "Okay, thank you, Corporal. You all right, lad?"

"Yeah," he replied. "I'm okay, sir."

"Good." I nodded.

"How's the gin situation, sir?" Harris asked quietly.

"Hm, we *are* getting rather low now," I told him. "I don't think that it'll last beyond tomorrow."

"Strewth!" he gasped.

"Mm. Indeed." I nodded. "There *must* be some around here, somewhere – even if it's bloody Belgian."

The long-awaited reinforcements finally arrived and replacements, for the chaps which we'd lost, were duly assigned.

Haversham

Those readers who are familiar with *The Bounder* will already be acquainted with the long-time thorn in my side that was Leighton Haversham. For everybody else; Haversham was a ghastly, irritating, self-aggrandising – but clueless and pitifully invertebrate – lame excuse for a human being. The awful, drawling, would-be fop was, needless to say, no pal of mine.

"Poncey! How the devil are you, old chap?" His hateful voice grated. "Still knocking-around with the old *Halibuteers* then, I see."

"Haversham," I sighed. "I thought that you were dead, old boy? Oh, no, it was just from the neck upwards, wasn't it?"

"Ha-ha-ha-ha! Nice one, Hugo!" he brayed. "Better that than dead from the waist down, eh? Actually, I've just been decorated again, you know."

"Really? New wallpaper at Haversham Hovel?"

"Ha-ha-ha! No, they only went and awarded me *another* CGM; it's becoming really embarrassing actually. Mind you, all the ladies *love* a soldier with big, shiny medals!" (For the dullards: a CGM is a Conspicuous Gallantry Medal.)

"Yes." I nodded. "Although they're sometimes just as taken with poor dumb animals."

"I'm up for a DDM too, you know."

Curiosity got the better of me. "DDM?" I frowned.

"Distinguished Dalliance Medal!" he leered, thrusting his pelvis back and forth.

"Ugh!" I tutted. "You see, now I just feel *ill*!"

"Why, I ought to form the 1st Debauchers Regiment!" he grinned stupidly. (Still performing the pelvic thrusts.)

"Ye-es." I sighed.

"The Household Dallianteers!"

"Aren't you supposed to *be* somewhere, Haversham?" I groaned. "Like having your skull drained or your spine stiffened or something?"

"Oh, but I've not yet told you about the Battle of Liège!" He frowned.

"Ah!" I nodded. "I knew that there must be a reason I was about to hang myself!"

"It was *the* most fabulous battle, Hugo," he declared. "You should have been there!"

"Yes, well, some of us…"

"No, you really *should* have been there; instead of hiding away down here in the forest like a load of simpering girls; we went right through their infantry like a dose of salts, you know!"

"Yes, well, of course their 7th Infantry Division is mostly made-up of the old and infirm, isn't it?"

"No, no! Fine soldiers; put up a hell of a fight they did!"

"Mm. Lethal at close range I would imagine; those walking sticks."

"Ha-ha-ha-ha!" Haversham guffawed. "I thought that *stick-warfare* was your halberdiers' department, actually!"

"Oh, touché, Leighton, old boy!" I exclaimed. "That's the stuff! I mean, I've heard it a thousand times before but you finally got there too, eh? Jolly well done!"

"Yes, well, I'm sorry that I can't hang around and hear all about your shameful pastings," he sneered. "But I have *got* to track-down some hot Belgian totty before my britches explode!"

"Well, it was *awful* to see you alive," I grimaced. "Look out for land mines won't you, old boy?"

"Ha-ha-ha-ha! Just let me know when you need to be rescued again, eh?" he drawled. "Love the 'tache too, by the way – it makes you look less of a git!"

"Die horribly, Haversham," I sneered.

"You too, old chap." He nodded.

"Eurgh! Who was *that*, sir?" Manning grimaced.

"*That*." I frowned. "Was Leighton bloody Haversham!"

"What a wanker!" Manning scowled. "Oh, sorry, sir, I mean, erm…"

"No you're quite right, Manning. Haversham is, as you have intimated, possessed of a most frightfully masturbatorial bent."

"What? He's a *poofter* an' all, sir?"

"No, I mean… Well, yes, he probably is, actually."

There were nearby cries of "Haversham!" and "Hurrah!" and I cringed. (*'Ugh!'*)

Operation Lifeline

I was only too glad when we received the order to return to Dinant and rendezvous with Colonel Brompton. The colonel had taken over Boothroyd's command headquarters and was seated in an office, again poring over a map of Belgium.

"Ah, Hugo." He beamed. "Congratulations, my boy!"

"Erm, on what, sir?" I shrugged.

"Why, on your little tank-hunting caper, of course! It was the perfect prelude to a splendid ambush and a beautifully orchestrated piece!"

"Oh, *that*, sir." I nodded. (I was reminded of Colonel Gainsborough, at Letchworth Military Academy, who likened the sounds of a ferocious battle to 'strange, beautiful music' and for whom command was entirely analogous to 'the conducting of a symphony orchestra'. Hmmm...)

"Jolly well done." Brompton winked. "You've given Jerry the jitters, good and proper; the Hun has retreated, back towards Ciney, with his tail between his legs!"

"Ha!" I sneered. "The spineless, sausage-eating bounders!"

"Yes, well now, I've been hearing some rather disconcerting things from a brigade HQ company further south, here in Beauraing," the colonel went on. "It seems that there's been quite a build-up of enemy infantry, of late. I'd like you to take your chaps for a drive down there, assess the situation, and see if you can't come up with another little Hun-scuppering caper, what?"

"Why, I'd be glad to, sir." I nodded. "And I know that the lads are as keen as mustard to see some more action."

"Good man," said Brompton. "Oh, and before you go, I managed to procure a small emergency supply of gin; to tide you over, as it were."

"Oh, jolly good show, sir!" I beamed. "We're damned-nearly out now."

"Yes, well, it came to me via some chaps up near Antwerp, you know. I'm afraid that it's, erm… Dutch."

"I'm sure that it'll be fine, sir," I replied, "I mean, they *invented* the stuff!"

"Mm. Well, there's only about half a dozen bottles here but, as I say, it ought to tide you over for a bit."

"I'm very grateful to you, sir." I nodded. "It's a load off my mind, I can tell you."

"Well, we can't have our chaps going without, now can we? I mean, God knows what might happen!"

"Hm." I frowned. "Indeed, sir."

I marched back outside and gathered the chaps around to explain to them where we would be going next and why, and an awful lot of groaning and complaining ensued. (Which is just the soldier's wont, I'm afraid. I've heard it said that it's only when they *stop* moaning that one needs to worry!)

"Shut up!" Harris snarled and the whining quickly abated.

"Come on now, lads," I urged, trying to enthuse them. "It's another opportunity for us to demonstrate our fearsome fighting abilities!" (There were a lot of 'Mmmms' and much shrugging.) "Let's show the rest of those rotten Nazis what British soldiers are made of!" (More shrugging.) "Ah! It must be time for some more gin then, eh?"

"Gin!" the lads cheered. "Hurrah!"

"Dole it out, Sergeant." I winked. "And let us drink to victory!"

"To victory!" the chaps cried. "HURRAH!"

With a nice little tot of gin in their bellies, the lads were back on top form and spoke loudly of their determination to utterly defeat, in mortal combat, the evil forces of Hitler. (They also – and quite worryingly – expressed the intention of decapitating any survivors and urinating down their necks. Hmmm…)

"That'd probably constitute a few violations of the Geneva Convention," I told them, with a disparaging frown. (They were, however, no less keen on the idea.)

The Rue de Beauraing bore the scarring of artillery shells too, and we did a lot of swerving-around-craters on the way. The further south we went, the hillier the landscape became, and ever more steep, narrow, tightly winding and muddy grew the roads. There were one or two difficult gradients, which involved some wheel-spins and the occasional bit of fart-inducing leg power, but at least that deep into the Ardennes there would not be the same threat from General Guderian's panzer divisions. (Or so it was thought!)

We arrived at a road junction to find a small army of bashed-up soldiers (Frenchies, Belgies, and British) all hastening westwards. I signalled the other drivers to halt and then dismounted.

"Where the hell are you, lot going?" I called out.

"Zer day is lost, *monsieur*," said one of the Frogs. "We 'ave no choice but to retreat."

"Don't be bloody ridiculous!" I scowled. "No battle was ever won by running away!"

"I implore you, Monsieur!" the Frenchie cried. "Retreat! Zer day is lost!"

"What did that Froggy say, sir?" asked one of the new lads.

"He said, Perkins, that he's a bloody spineless pant-shitter!" I replied with another scowl.

"May we dismount, sir?" asked Hawkins.

"Yep, might as well I suppose." I nodded. "Who needs a clear-out? Let's have a show of hands." (Most of the chaps indicated the need.) "Right, well, I don't want you disappearing-off all at once," I told them, "so you can go in groups of four. Sa'nt Harris, organise that, would you?"

"Yessah!" said Harris. "Right, first crapper detail; Hawkins, Ferguson, Tucker and Davenport, off you go – and be quick about it, too!" (The quartet scurried-off into the woods.)

"You there!" I shouted at a passing Tommy. "That man!"

(The young soldier looked filthy, battered, and exhausted.) "Sir?" He frowned.

"What's going on here, Private? Who's in command?"

The lad looked around. "I reckon that'd be *you*, sir," he replied.

"Oh," I sighed. "Well, you're all going the wrong way!"

"Everyone's pulling-back to Jeuville, sir," he said. "We got ambushed by a tank outside of Beauraing and our CO, Lieutenant Merryweather, got killed; I think there's still some chaps cut-off, back down the road there."

"How many?"

"I dunno, sir." He shrugged. "You'd better 'ave a word wiv the Froggies; if you can get any bloody sense out of 'em."

"What's your name, Soldier?" I asked him.

"81326 Private William Gantry, sir."

"What's the strength of the Jerry forces in Beauraing then, Gantry?"

"Several divisions, sir," he replied. "Some of 'em SS."

"Ugh!" I tutted. "All right, Private, that'll be all, lad," (I waved my map at one of the Frenchies.) "Hey, *garçon!*"

"*Oui, monsieur?*" He replied, squinting through little rectangular spectacles.

I showed the shabby fellow the map. "There are men cut-off, down this road, oui? There is a tank?"

"*Oui, monsieur*," he drawled. "Zer tank is in ziss lane, 'ere, I sink." (He prodded a filthy, trembling finger at the map.) "Zer men dare not move from zeir position and zer Germans will soon be advancing from Beauraing."

"Well, don't you think that it would be a good idea to go and get those chaps out of there?" I scowled.

"*Oui, monsieur*." He nodded. "But, sir, none of us 'as any fight left in 'im."

"Huh!" I scoffed. "Well, my chaps have plenty!"

Once all of the lads' lavatorial needs had been met, and Harris had taken a quick headcount, I spread the map out on the ground and explained the situation; stressing that there may be *British* troops in trouble. (And not just a load of worthless, whiffy Frenchies!)

"I shall be leading a four-man team on an assault of the panzer position," I told them, as I filled empty gin bottles with petrol. "When the armour has been dispatched, a second team, led by Sergeant Harris, will go in and evacuate the stranded chaps. All clear?" (There was a chorus of affirmatives.) "Corporal Manning will lead the remainder of the platoon to Jeuville and take-up defensive positions, on this side of the river, and wait for the rest of us there. Sergeant Harris?"

"Sir?"

"Dole out some more gin."

"Hurrah!" The lads cheered.

Harris distributed gin amongst the lads and then came over to me. "Where on earth did you get it from, sir?" He asked. "I thought we was out."

"Colonel Brompton managed to lay hands on some," I replied. "It's Dutch though, so I put it into one of our empties."

"Shrewd, sir." The sergeant winked. "I thought it tasted different. Do you think they'll notice?"

"Your guess is as good as mine, Sergeant." I shrugged. "It *does* taste rather different, doesn't it?"

(The effect of 'Dutch Courage' on the chaps was extraordinary, profound, and startling.)

"Where's them bastard Jerries then, sir?" Miggs glared. "I'll stick this flippin' bayonet right up 'em!"

"Yeah, let's 'ave 'em, sir!" Manning seethed. "The rotten Nazi bastards!"

"Mm." I nodded. "That's the spirit, chaps."

"Wankers!" Davenport scowled. "Sausage-eatin' wankers!"

(The potvaliancy conferred by Dutch gin was extreme, and the lads were certain to fight furiously on the fearsome stuff!) I took another little nip of the *Graandhollandse*

Jenever myself. "Ooh!" I shuddered. "Extraordinary! Right, let's go and slaughter some bloody Krauts then, eh?"

"HURRAARGH!" the lads roared, a fire of madness in their eyes.

(*'Strewth!'* I gasped to myself. *'Fearsome!'*)

I reversed Nelly down the road and parked-up at our rendezvous point. The squad then separated into its two four-man sections; Harris, Miggs, Davenport and Trubshaw continued down the road whilst I led Tucker, Roberts and Hinckley northwards into the woods, for fifty yards, and then turned due east.

"As long as we stay on this heading," I told my lads, "we ought to come out right on top of that swine panzer."

We picked our way, slowly and cautiously, through the dense coniferous woodland, until the tank was spotted.

"His turret's pointing towards the road but he's front-on to us, sir," Tucker whispered, peering through the sight on his Boys rifle. "Even this bugger won't get through three inches of steel. Shall I try to get around behind 'im, sir?"

"No, forget that," I replied. "I doubt very much that we have the time. Two of us will go down there and give him a couple of petrol bombs and a grenade; when the crew dismounts, the other two can finish 'em off."

Private Roberts and I crawled on our bellies into position at the edge of the wood and lit our wicks. I gave him the nod and we both lobbed our incendiaries. The sound of glass smashing was followed by a loud "WHOOMF!" as the tank was engulfed in flames. I could hear the Panzer's turret rotating as I tossed a grenade underneath it and hit the deck with my arms covering my head. BOOM!

Screaming, burning Jerries tumbled from the stricken vehicle and were quickly cut down by Tubby's elephant gun and small-arms fire from Hinckley, Roberts and myself.

Back at the RV, there were thirty or forty bashed-up Frenchies, all armed with old, Froggy *Modèle* 1886 Lebel rifles (and all with the same strange, musty and unsavoury odour about them), but of Harris's section there was no sign.

One of the shabby Frogs approached me with a sloppy salute. "*Oh, monsieur!*" He blubbered. "*Mon Dieu!*"

"Not quite," I replied (demonstrating a *proper* salute). "Hugo Poncenby; First Halberds."

"I am André Dauphinois of zer Brigade of Republican Fauchardiers," the Frenchie drawled. "Monsieur, zere is a sniper! One of your men took a bullet, I sink."

"Oh, great." I tutted. "All right, well, you fellows better fall-back to Jeuville, eh? And make sure that no one blows-up that bloody bridge just yet!"

"*Oui, monsieur.*" He nodded. "I will make sure of ziss."

My section continued down the road and soon found Davenport and Trubshaw cowering behind a hedge.

"Where are Harris and Miggs?" I asked Davenport.

"Sa'nt Harris is pinned-down by a sniper, just around the corner, sir," he replied. "I'm afraid I dunno about Miggsy."

I ventured a little further and spied Harris slumped in the shadow of a low wall. "Harris?" I hissed.

"Stay there, sir!" he gasped. "There's a sniper!"

"I know about the sniper," I told him. "Are you hit?"

"Right leg, sir," he replied. "He got Miggsy in the 'ead I think he's… I think he's dead, sir."

"Do you know where the sniper is?"

"There are some farm buildings, to the south there, sir. I think the shots came from one of them."

"Okay." I nodded. "I'm going to go and take a peek; hold on there and keep your head down, eh?"

I scurried southwards, along a rather sparse and scraggy hedgerow, until I could see the group of buildings in question. The swine sniper had made a stupid, schoolboy error; through field glasses, one could just make out the barrel of his Mauser Karibiner 98K rifle protruding through a hole in the tiled roof of the farmhouse.

"Gotcha!" I scowled. "He's in the farmhouse," I told the chaps, "Up in the attic."

"I can't get a shot on 'im from 'ere, sir," said Tubby, peering through his scope. "Should I get a better position?"

"No," I replied, "he's bound to spot you if you move out any further. I'll have to try and get around behind him."

"Go careful eh, sir," said Davenport.

"Ha-ha! Don't you worry about me, lad." I winked. (I do have to confess, though, that my bum was doing that twitching thing again!)

I worked my way along the hedgerow and around to the back of the farmhouse. There were plenty of holes in the roof, through which a grenade would fit, though none of them was very large. (It was a one-shot proposition; if I missed, and the grenade fell outside, then the Nazi swine would be alerted to my presence; if I could just manage to get it in through one of those holes though…)

I took a deep breath, and eyed-up my target, then pulled the pin from a hand grenade and 'cooked' it for a couple of seconds before hurling it high into the air. I gave a little gasp and held my breath as, just for a moment, it looked like it was going to fall-short. ("Pffrt!" went my backside.)

In the event, though, it dropped neatly through the hole in the roof and exploded a moment later. The fate of the sniper was in no doubt either; he was blown out of the attic and fell, with a nasty crunch, in a smouldering heap on the front path.

I crept up for a look and grimaced at the state the young Jerry was in; he was severely burned and had terrible shrapnel wounds in his face and chest; moreover, his spine was horribly twisted from the fall and his entire frame mangled-looking. (His bowels had emptied too and he reeked!) He was groaning and gurgling horrifically through the crimson froth which poured from his smashed face, so I slipped the catch on my revolver and put a round in his head before scarpering to Harris's position.

"Where's Miggsy then?" I asked the sergeant.

"He went down over there somewhere," Harris replied, pointing. "I reckon he's had it though, sir. He copped one in the noggin."

Jerry machine gun fire suddenly broke-out to the south of us.

"Come on; let's get out of here, sir!" Tucker urged.

"We're not going anywhere without Miggs," I told him.

"But he's dead, sir."

"No one gets left behind!" I insisted. "Trubshaw; help the sergeant back to the truck."

"Yes, sir."

"The rest of you, give me some cover."

"Yes, sir," said Davenport, positioning himself on his belly with one of the LMGs. The others took-up positions and they all began to fire in the direction of the advancing enemy.

I scampered along the edge of the field, with Jerry rounds whizzing overhead, until I found Miggs; he was lying on his back with blood covering half of his face. I couldn't tell whether he was breathing or not but when I held his wrist and put my fingertips to his radial artery, to my great relief, I felt a pulse. I grabbed him by his webbing and dragged his carcass towards the others, all the time firing my revolver wildly behind me. ("Pfft!" went my twitching backside.)

"Christ! There's bloody 'undreds of 'em, sir!" Davenport scowled.

"Right." I panted. "It's probably time that we made ourselves scarce then, yes?"

Still firing wildly, we withdrew to the rendezvous point. The lads hoisted Miggs's limp body into the back of the gin palace and Roberts whipped-out his medic kit. I scrambled up into the cab and, under another hail of bloody machine gun fire, the Ford truck fought its way over the brow of the hill, and we were borne out of harm's way – for the time being.

Bridge Over the River Meuse

Jeuville was a shabby little town, even by Belgie standards; a couple of dozen timber-built cottages and three-up-two-down houses (some of which looked like they dated from as far back as the seventeenth century) clustered around a simple, hump-backed, arch bridge made of limestone blocks.

I located the rest of the platoon and parked-up nearby.

"Oh you made it, sir!" Manning gasped. "Thank Christ for that! The Froggies said there was a sniper."

"Yes." I frowned. "He got the sergeant in the leg and poor old Miggsy in the head."

(Miggs had been incredibly fortunate actually; the sniper's bullet had split-open his ginger scalp and left him with a big lump but had not, it seemed, penetrated his thick cranium.)

"Ooh," he groaned, as he began to regain consciousness. "What can I get for two-and-six?"

"Hmmm." I frowned. "Are you *with* us, Private?"

He opened one eye. "Oh," he said, "erm…what was you just sayin' there?"

"Hold still," I told him. "You've had a bit of a whack on the old noggin. Do you know where you are, lad?"

Miggs thought for a moment. "Erm…oh yeah." He tutted. "Bloody Belgium, sir!"

"Ha!" I chuckled. "Welcome back, Miggsy!"

"Mm. You're gonna need a stitch or two in that," Roberts told him as he cleaned around Miggs's wound.

"Ow!" Miggs winced, sucking air in through his teeth.

Sergeant Harris was looking deathly pale and very poorly indeed; his skin was cold, and clammy to the touch, and he seemed to be fading in and out of consciousness.

"I've fixed him up, sir," Roberts sighed. "But he's already lost rather a lot of blood; we really need to get some saline in him."

"I'm ever-so sorry, sir," Harris mumbled, "but I'm afraid that I seem to have pissed myself!"

"Least of your worries, old boy." I shrugged.

"Ugh!" he suddenly groaned, his eyes rolling in their sockets. "Oh bugger!" ("Pffffrrrt!" went his rear.)

"Harris?" I frowned.

"Sarge!" Manning cried.

"Stay with us, Harris!" I told him. "Do you hear me, Sergeant?"

Moments later though (and despite everybody's very best efforts), my sergeant, 91312 Anthony Wilfred Harris, was dead.

"Shit!" I seethed. "Right, that's bloody-well *it*! We shall make a stand, right here."

"Erm…is that wise, sir?" asked Manning.

"No," I replied, shaking my head. "It's not wise. Nor is it even very sensible."

"So, why, er…?"

"Because it is *necessary*," I told him. "Apart from anything else, there's so much traffic bottle-necked on the approach to the bridge that we're going to need to buy a little time for it to clear."

I was organising the lads into defensive positions when there came a drawling Froggy voice which rang a little chime of recognition. "Oh, Capitaine Poncenby!" it gabbled. "Sank God I 'ave found you, *monsieur*!"

"Ah." I smiled. "It's Captain, erm… *Dolphin-wah*, isn't it?"

"I was told zat you are mounting zer rearguard action, *monsieur*?" Dauphinois frowned.

"Yes." I nodded. "It ought to buy you fellows a little extra time to fall-back across the bridge."

"Ziss is very 'eroic of you, sir!" he exclaimed.

"No," I sighed. "It's just rather unavoidable."

"I 'ave ziss for you, Capitaine," he said, handing me a strange, stubby bottle of brown-orange liquid with the word *COURVOISIER* on the label. "It is a very good cognac."

"Con-yack, eh?" I smiled weakly. "Well, yes, thank you very much, Captain."

Dauphinois gave a sigh. "My men are moving-out, *monsieur*," he said. "I'm afraid zat I must be leaving very soon also."

"Well, it was jolly nice to see you again," I lied. "Thanks awfully for the old Con-yack, eh."

"You and your men 'ave my undying admiration, sir," he sobbed (offering a *fair* salute only). "You are all bloody 'eroes!"

"No." I smiled, saluting properly. "We're all bloody *British*!" (Why *do* the Froggies blub like that, eh?)

I went to the gin palace, stashed the cognac, and fetched the last bottle of Dutch Courage.

"Sa'nt Harris…" (I stopped myself and let out a sigh.) "Manning; dole-out the gin, would you, lad?"

"Yes, sir." He nodded, sighing mournfully also.

My new platoon sergeant distributed the gin and there followed a lot of growling, swearing, and gnashing of teeth.

"Right, chaps." I scowled. "Let's give these bloody filthy Nazis what-for, eh?"

"Hurr-aargh!" the lads snarled. (*'Hmmm…'*)

The Jerry infantry commenced its advance – and marched right into our minefields.

"Ha-ha! You Teutonic tossers!" Ferguson sneered, laying-into the enemy with LMG fire.

"Come on!" Davenport scowled. "You sausage-eatin' Nazi wankers!"

The battle for Jeuville was fierce and bloody but, eventually, the numbers of enemy infantry slowly began to dwindle.

"I'm out, sir!" Ferguson declared, yanking the empty magazine from his Bren gun and dropping it to the ground.

"Me too, sir," said Davenport.

"Tubbs?" I enquired.

(BANG! went Tucker's Boys rifle.) "Yep." He nodded. "That was my last round an' all, sir."

"All right, fix bayonets," I said calmly. "Stay hidden and wait for my order."

For those readers who may not know: the halberd is a pole arm, anywhere between five and eight feet in length, at whose business-end is a long, steel spike for stabbing; a curved axe blade for hacking; and, usually, a backward-pointing barb of some kind. (Wonderful for hooking into the back of an enemy's neck and severing his spine!) Historically, the halberds-man was an infantryman who specialised in the use of such weapons, and the well-trained halberds-man was a foot soldier greatly to be feared.

A Lee Enfield rifle, with fixed bayonet, is also a very tasty weapon indeed for close-quarters fighting. (I do not propose, herein, to describe the various techniques and disciplines involved but let it suffice to say that, in the hands of a competent Halberdier, it is especially lethal; any opponent within a ten-foot radius, who has not already taken-aim, is a bloody dead man!)

The lads held their nerve, and kept their heads down, as a group of a dozen Jerry infantrymen started to pick their way, down the grotty little Belgie street, towards our positions.

"Sir?" Manning whispered.

"Not yet, lad," I told him.

The Nazi troops continued to work their way towards us.

"Now, sir?"

"Not yet…"

The rotten swine were almost upon us.

"Sir?"

"Now." I nodded. "For England!"

"Charge!" Cried Manning.

"Aargh!" Tucker screamed.

"Wankers!" yelled Davenport.

The despicable Nazi swine didn't know what the bloody hell had hit them; from every direction, cold British steel thrust, stabbed, and slashed its way into their ranks until the street was awash with Jerry blood, and filled with such an intense and overwhelming stink of rotting cabbage, that even the most seasoned of the chaps (myself included) vomited uncontrollably.

"Eurgh! I can *taste* it!" Hawkins gagged.

"Heurp!" I retched. "I can't bloody breathe!"

"My eyes!" Tucker wailed. "Aargh! My eyes!"

"Everybody fall-back!" I belched. "Fall... (heurp)...back!"

We hastily withdrew from the danger-zone and regrouped. (The effects of even a short exposure to such high concentrations of stinking Jerry nastiness were powerful and debilitating, and it was a good ten minutes before everyone had finally stopped throwing-up.)

"Jesus!" I gasped. "If we ever decide to do that again, let's remember to put our gas masks on first, agreed?"

"Too bloody right, sir!" Manning retched. "Heurp!"

"Oh, my God!" Davenport spluttered as he lay on the ground, panting for breath. "That was poison, sir... *Poison!*"

"Is everyone all right?" I asked.

"I think I've got a bit o' follow-through in my pants, sir," Hawkins grimaced.

"Nemmind." I shrugged. "I wouldn't worry too much about that, lad. Everybody else recovering okay?"

(It seemed that, on-the-whole, they were.)

"Oh, sir." Roberts scowled. "I've never smelt anything so 'orrible as that in all my bloody life!"

"The potency of their foul stench is obviously proportional to the depth of their Nazi rottenness," I *reasoned*. "Did you see the bounders' uniforms? Those swine were hard-core *Schutz-Staffel*."

"Shit-stuffers, sir?" Hawkins gasped.

I shook my head and sighed. "Waffen-SS, lad."

"Eurgh! SS?" He glared. "Rotten bastards!"

"How many mortar rounds do we have, Corp...*Sergeant*?" I asked Manning.

"Erm...oh..." (His shoulders sagged.) "One, sir," he replied.

"One?" I tutted. "Oh God. What about hand grenades?"

"Erm...two, sir, by the looks of it; plus whatever *you*'ve got left."

"Hm. That still only equals two then, I'm afraid."

"Ooh, there's still a petrol bomb, sir!" said Ferguson.

"No." I frowned. "I think that we may need to press the contents of that into service for the rather novel and unorthodox purpose of fuelling our internal combustion engines."

"Oh, yeah." He nodded.

"What we gonna do then, sir?" Manning sighed. "We can't bayonet the lot of 'em."

"No," I agreed, "quite so. But I'm afraid that we have another rather serious problem, too."

"What's that then, sir?"

"Well," I said solemnly. "The fact of the matter is that, erm...well, there's no more gin left either."

There came a collective gasp. (And a few deplorable – if very imaginative – profanities.)

"No!" Manning exclaimed. "Oh my God!"

("Pffrt!" went Tucker's britches.)

"I know." I nodded. "Come on now, lads; let's keep it together, eh? There's still a bottle of Con-yack, which the Frenchies left us, as an emergency back-up."

"Con-yack, sir?" Ferguson grimaced. "It's not made from snails, is it?"

"No, you're all right, lad." I winked. "This is a non-snail variety."

"It still sounds like puke to me," Davenport muttered.

There was a sudden, loud roaring of engines as a dozen Panzers broke-cover and came crashing out of the pine woods, in line-formation, with all guns blazing.

"Now, where the bloody hell did *they* come from?" I gasped.

"Incoming!" Manning yelled, diving to the floor.

"BANG!" The whole bloody street shook as one of their main guns brought down a building across the road. Several of the armoured monstrosities fell-foul of our anti-tank mines, and their charge lost its momentum, but the remaining Panzers continued to pound everything in their ruddy sight until an artillery bombardment, from across the river, forced them to withdraw.

"Roberts, Madeley and Large copped it, sir," Manning reported. "Madeley's lost a leg and an arm, sir. He's alive, at the moment, but I don't fancy his chances."

"I see." I nodded. "What about Private Large; is he going to be all right?"

"No, sir. He's got some bits missing too." Manning grimaced. "And Trubshaw reckons that it's probably part of Madeley's femur that's sticking out of his eye."

"Oh." I frowned (fighting-off the urge to spew). "How about Roberts?"

"He was fatally wounded, sir, when a tube of antiseptic cream from the medical kit pierced his liver at some considerable velocity."

"Good grief!"

"Mm. Pretty ironic eh, sir; a medic bein' killed by a tube o' Savlon?"

"Hmmm." I nodded. "That *is* pretty bloody ironic."

I sent a few of the chaps out on the scrounge but all that they managed to bag was a 250-round belt of Browning ammo and a couple more hand grenades.

"Right, I think that the road has now cleared enough to make a run for it," I told everyone. "Get Bertha and Gertrude across the bridge, quick-smart!"

"What about you and Nelly, sir?" asked Hawkins.

"Somebody is going to have to cover your withdrawal," I told him.

(There came a lot of mumbling and unwarranted discourse.)

"Shut up, you lot!" Manning snapped.

(*"Good lad!"* I smiled to myself.) "Davenport, since you're the new corporal, you'll drive Gertrude."

"Right-ho, sir." He nodded.

Away to the east, more small arms fire erupted and the panzers' V-12 Maybach engines could be heard revving.

"Come on, sir," Manning urged. "The artillery across the river can keep us covered."

"Just fall back across the bridge, eh?" I frowned.

"Not without you, sir," he said. "The Frogs are gonna blow it up, any minute!"

"I appreciate the sentiment." I nodded. "But I shall provide covering fire for the rest of you, whilst you cross the bridge, and I will require cover from you lot when I withdraw, hm? So *you* had better get your stubborn, insubordinate backside over that damned bridge, lad – or else!"

"All right, sir." Manning tutted. "But I want it to be known that I strongly object."

"Objection duly noted, Sergeant." I chuckled. "Now, clear-off! I'll be right behind you."

"Right behind us, sir?"

"Just bugger off, will you?"

After parking Nelly within reasonable scarpering distance, I hooked the handful of precious grenades onto my webbing and set-up one of the Browning LMGs at the position which I had selected. I gave the lads their signal to move out and opened-up with the LMG.

Three-inch and five-inch artillery shells, fired from British howitzers on the other side of the river, whistled overhead and pounded the middle-distance, keeping the armour at bay, but the eastern edge of the town was already crawling with stinking Jerry infantry. I squirted the LMG with my left hand, so that the Browning sporadically sprayed .303 rounds down the street, and used my teeth to pull the pin from a grenade, which I held in my right; I let the grenade cook for a couple of seconds and then lobbed it, in a sweeping overarm motion, in the vague direction of the approaching enemy. Having repeated this process – until the two trucks were out of earshot, the grenades were gone, and the Browning had spat-out every last one of the 250 rounds on the belt – I beat a very hasty bloody retreat. (The pair of battered, old Commer Q4s were, in the event, the last vehicles ever to trundle over that lichen-encrusted, nineteenth-century stone bridge.)

I was about to clamber into Nelly's cab when I caught a sudden bright flash, out of the corner of my eye, and instinctively hit the deck. The truck took a direct hit from a bloody 50 mm explosive tank round and pieces of shrapnel, and smouldering fragments of the Ford F2, filled the air and began to rain-down all around. The bloody wily Hun had launched a surprise flanking attack from the south; in the near-distance, a pall of smoke rose into the air as the flame-throwers moved in and the panzers, away to the east – despite our artillery – once again began to advance on the town. Faced with this sobering reality I picked myself up, dusted myself down, and then scarpered away into the woods for my ruddy life.

"Halt!" cried a Jerry voice somewhere behind me. *"Englander – halt!"*

"Not bloody likely!" I winced as MG34s and Mauser rifles sent bullets whizzing past me and thwacking into the trees all around.

In my haste to flee though, I'd failed to notice a broken lower branch which was sticking out at head-height; and which subsequently left several large splinters of pine embedded in my right cheek. "Bastard!" I seethed as I leapt to my feet and took-off again. (An inch or so higher and it would have taken my sodding eye out!) I could feel my cheek swelling-up by the second as I ran, but at least the stabbing pains soon subsided and gave-way to a dull, aching throb.

I fancied that I might be approaching a little clearing in the trees when the ground suddenly vanished from beneath my feet and I found myself tumbling down one of the many little gullies which feed into the Meuse. (It was not the manner in which one would have chosen to descend to the river but it very quickly put some distance between myself and my pursuers.) "SPLOSH!"

For a moment or two, I could hear nothing but the deafening roar of the foaming white waters. (Which, incidentally, were bloody-well freezing!) "Jesus C-Christ!" I gasped, as I battled with the fearsome currents, struggling to catch my breath. Rifle shots and daft Germanese babbling echoed across the valley, and bullets began to whiz by and plop into the water, as the river swept me away northwards, and I swore loudly when a stray round tore a chunk out of my right shoulder: "Ow! Shit!"

Though it can only have taken a couple of minutes to fight my way to the opposite bank, it seemed like a ruddy eternity. My main problem then was finding a spot where I could bloody-well clamber out again. A solution presented itself though, when I suddenly slammed into a huge, half-submerged boulder (and was damn-nearly KO'd by the impact). Clinging onto the slippery rock, I briefly put a hand to my head and frowned at the blood on my palm. "Bugger!" I groaned.

The knock on the old bonce had left me feeling a little woozy but I was at least conscious, and able to drag myself from the churning waters, up onto the hunk of weathered stone, to make a desperate lunge for the bank. (It wasn't, perhaps, the most agile or elegant of leaps (or landings) and was certainly far outclassed – in terms of distance alone – by the legendary horse of Dinant; there are doubtless those who, had they been there to witness it, might possibly describe it as having been ungainly...*clumsy* even. I was, however, across the bloody Meuse and back on *terra firma*.)

From back up the river came the sound of loud, booming explosions and, soon after that, bits of floating debris came sweeping past. The bridge at Jeuville had been destroyed and the Nazi advance there temporarily halted.

I desperately wanted to lay down and rest but knew that, were I to lose consciousness, I might never get up again, so I hastily dressed my shoulder and bandaged my aching head, vomited, and then clambered-off up the side of the valley. (It was imperative that I re-joined the chaps at once; exactly what the bloody hell they might get up to, without an officer to keep them in line, just didn't bear thinking about!)

I could probably just about make it back to Jeuville before nightfall...perhaps. My map showed the contours of the landscape accurately enough for me to plan a route which circumnavigated any tall, steep hills (the smaller, sprawling ones being less arduous and traversable directly.) The numerous waterways, though, were another matter entirely; the smaller streams were fairly easy to negotiate but the rivers often required quite a lengthy detour before they could be crossed in even relative safety. (Where they were broad and shallow, for example, or by utilising one of the many, but precarious, natural bridges formed by fallen trees.)

The smell of woodlands – of damp earth, leaf mould and flowering plants – must, I think, be deeply ingrained into the human psyche. If one takes the time to close one's eyes and flare one's nostrils, to slowly fill one's lungs with the fragrant arboreal air, and let the myriad subtle aromas percolate through one's mind, then you probably have a good deal too much time on your hands.

The woods *were* always like a second home to me though and, as a boy, I spent innumerable blissful hours – alone or in company – shooting birds; trapping small animals; lighting fires; and generally pillaging Mother Nature of her bountiful harvest! (Hmmm, now that I *see* those words which I just hammered casually into the surface of the paper... Hmmm...)

Anyway, off I trudged southwards, over a thick, springy carpet of dead, rusty-brown, pine needles. The rest of the flora was sparse and pretty unremarkable: the occasional nettle, dandelion or cowslip; docks, bracken; and stands of willow herb. A fat wood pigeon sat on a branch and cooed loudly as smaller birds – tree pipits, finches and the like – flitted here and there, twittering madly; and bushy-tailed squirrels chased each other about amongst the trees.

Midges are generally divided into two families: Ceratopogonidae, the biting midges that suck blood, and the non-biting Chironomidae. The little buggers with which the Ardennes seemed to be swarming at that time were definitely very thirsty examples of the former, and I was soon covered in itchy, irritating bites.

I had heard the swirling and splashing of the waters long before I came upon the river; it was one of the innumerable tributaries which drained into the Meuse and, though not particularly deep, it was *very* fast-flowing. I worked my way a little further upstream and soon found a spot where a fallen tree had bridged the waterway. It was rather close to the frothing surface, and therefore a bit wet and slippery, but it was the only such crossing-point which I could see anywhere along that stretch.

I could have simply slipped from the tree and fallen into the river but, no; I had to come down astride the damned thing – taking the full force on my poor testes. I then listed, slowly and inexorably, to my right, before finally losing the battle with gravity and sliding off altogether. "Splash!" I was in the bloody drink again.

"Bloody, bastard and buggery!" I cursed.

This waterway, whilst every bit as cold as the Meuse, was not nearly so perilously torrential though and I was able, with care, to wade to the other bank and extricate myself without too much trouble.

My estimations proved to be even more wildly optimistic than I'd imagined. I had still not reached Jeuville by the time that the sun sank in the west and, as the light began to fade, the temperature started to plummet. I was going to have to make camp, and risk lighting a small fire, in order to keep warm and to dry my sodden clothing. (Or *sodding* clothing, if you prefer; either works!)

A long, long time ago, our ancient ancestors discovered a secret; it was a secret which came to set *Homo sapiens* apart from all other beasts; a secret which enabled humans to more easily extract the nutrients from their food, to ward-off dangerous creatures, to see in the dark, and to reduce each other to ashes. In the mythology of Ancient Greece, it was Prometheus who stole the secret of fire from the gods and brought it here to Earth for mankind. The secret was taught to me when I was very young and I firmly believe that it is something which every person ought to possess. It is for this reason that I shall now take a moment to share it with any queer readers whose notice it may have escaped. The *secret* of fire is that combustion requires heat, fuel, and oxygen, in varying proportions. That's it. (What? You didn't think that I was about to tell you how to get a bloody fire going, did you? Try rubbing two boy scouts together, you dullards!)

Ahem. Now then, the rest of us…where was I? Ah, yes; *the night was clear and cold…*

The night was clear and cold and the inky-black sky filled with countless brilliant, twinkling stars. I shook the residual

Meuse water from my boots, and my pipe, and spread the soggy baccy out by the fire. Everything else – clothes, socks and underwear – I hung on sticks around the little hearth. Since I had a fire going, and was surrounded by pine cones, I heated a couple of mature ones until they opened-up, releasing their seeds, and spent some time removing the shells and nibbling on the tiny nuts inside.

I simply couldn't bear sitting there in nothing but my webbing though and, whilst my underwear was still damp (and, I have to say, a bit frightful-looking), I felt equally daft, but a little less vulnerable, once my pants were back on.

'Flash-drying' the tobacco hadn't done it any favours but at least some of it was now smokable again and I huddled close to the fire with my pipe, occasionally turning my clothes until they were dry enough to wear. (I had, of course, already started sniffling and bloody sneezing by then though!)

I was rather surprised to hear voices, a little later, and my first thought was that it must be a ruddy Nazi patrol. (I was, then, greatly perplexed when a veritable multitude of shabby Belgie peasants suddenly came blundering, in a blind panic, right into my bloody camp.)

"Mon Dieu!" exclaimed one of the scruffy, whiffy fellows when he noticed me lying there.

"Hugo Poncenby," I told him, sitting upright. "I'm with the British Exp…"

"You must flee ziss place, *monsieur!*" He scowled, looking over his shoulder. "Zer enemy's dragon is burning everysing wiz its fire!"

"*Dragon*?" I sneered. "What the hell are you talking about?"

There was a crackling noise in the distance and a faint whiff of acrid smoke came to my nostrils.

Most of the scrag-bag Belgies were in a terrible bloody state; there were some serious burns amongst them, and all kinds of other horrendous injuries besides. (I wondered, frankly, how most of them were still alive at all as they looked, to me, like a load of walking bloody corpses!)

The smoke thickened, the crackling grew louder, and the forest was illuminated by an eerie orange glow.

"Zer dragon, *monsieur*!" the Belgie babbled. "Run for your life!"

"Don't be absurd!" I told him. "There's no bloody dragon!"

Through the trees to the east, where wailing Belgies frantically scattered this-way-and-that, burned the strangest fire that I'd ever seen; one by one, trees spontaneously burst into flames and then each appeared to crumble to cinders and ash within seconds.

"What the…?" (I could only surmise that the filthy Hun had unleashed a terrible new secret weapon; some kind of horrific 'death-ray' which was – even as I stood there, aghast – incinerating and *disintegrating* everything around me.) "Jesus Christ!" I coughed, as the scalding heat began to peel my blistering skin and scorching air seared the lining of my lungs.

Then, out of the raging inferno, came the strangest and most terrifying apparition that I have ever witnessed in my bloody life: a gigantic pair of glaring eyes and an enormous, gaping maw – filled with rows of huge, razor-sharp teeth – was bearing down on me and about to bite my sodding head right off! (I then awoke with a sudden, violent start.) "Bloody hell!" I gasped, drawing a sharp breath.

I sat up and yawned, ran my fingers through my hair, and gave a sigh. I didn't feel much like going back to sleep after that, so I laid a loose handful of dry twigs on the fire and blew gently until the few remaining embers began to glow orange and the twigs ignited. Before long, dawn broke and the damned birds started shrieking at each other. (I'm not averse to birdsong of course – some have a very pretty little repertoire indeed – I could just have used a bit more kip and was rather annoyed at the recent turn of events, that's all.) I felt a little less ratty by the time that I had a bit of a brew on the go.

The morning was pleasant enough; some hill fog persisted early on but, by the time that the sun had climbed a little higher into the sky, it was shaping-up to be a fine day. Having made certain that the fire was properly extinguished, I packed-up my gear, and removed all traces of my having been there.

The European boar *Sus scrofa* of the family Suidae, from which the domesticated pig varieties derive, is a stout and sturdy beast, up to four and a half feet long and three feet high, with some really quite formidable tusks at its disposal. They are mainly woodland-dwelling and, ordinarily, of fairly gregarious nature, feeding on roots and nuts or insects and sometimes carrion.

This particular specimen was little more than a piglet really. As I watched it snuffle around the base of a tree, grunting, and occasionally kicking at the ground with its trotter, I couldn't help but picture the little bugger glazed with honey and turning slowly on a spit, over hot coals. When another one wandered into view, I began to wonder if perhaps

Mummy Boar might not be lurking somewhere nearby and, moments later, there she was; about a hundred and forty pounds of succulent, wild pig. Mmm!

I was in no way positioned between the sow and her piglets, nor blocking any conceivable escape route. Nevertheless, Mrs Boar seemed very displeased at my presence in her part of the forest, and was quickly becoming very agitated.

"I'll admit that I *am* a little peckish," I told her gently, "but you've really nothing to fear from me."

She snorted and started stamping her trotters and tearing-up the ground around her. (The piglets scurried-off out of sight.) I slowly lifted my right boot a couple of inches from the ground and gently set it back down again behind me. The boar suddenly made a sort of half-charge but I managed to hold my nerve and she stopped and stood there, grunting, snorting, stamping, and glaring at me hatefully. I made no eye-contact, but kept her in my peripheral vision, as I slowly moved my left foot backwards. "That's it, keep your wig on, madam," I said quietly. "Nice and easy, now…"

I'd already formulated an escape plan, in case she decided to make a *proper* charge, and seconds later I put it into operation when she came thundering towards me – clearly with every intention of slicing some part of me wide open. I looked down at her from the branch to which I was clinging and laughed. "Ha! Now, sod-off and look after those piglets of yours," I sneered. "You, walking pork-banquet!"

Whether she knew that her little ones were safely hidden nearby, and was determined to vent her fury on me – or was so focussed on doing me harm that she'd forgotten all about them – the bloody sow made it quite clear that she was going nowhere, any time soon, so I clambered onto a sturdier branch, loaded-up the briar, and sat there smoking while she circled the tree, digging at its roots with those savage-looking tusks.

By the time that three-quarters of an hour had elapsed, I'd grown completely bloody sick of being perched in a tree and was threatening the stupid boar with my revolver. "I'll do it!" I told her. "You might have a family and all that but, so-help-me, I'll put a bloody bullet right between your eyes in a minute, you stupid pig!"

She eyed me casually from where she was lying in the shade of a clump of bracken.

"Are you mentally defective?" I tutted.

Whatever her porcine reason may have been, she chose that precise moment to heave herself up onto her trotters (and shoot me a last, contemptuous glare) before sauntering-off into the woods without looking back. I waited for a minute or two before lowering myself to the ground and listening intently; all that I could hear though was the mad twittering of the birds, the whispering of the wind in the trees, and the faint, distant thudding of artillery shells.

I hiked the rest of the way back up the valley to Jeuville, only to find that most of the Allied forces had buggered-off elsewhere, leaving a handful of Frenchies behind to man an observation post.

"Where the hell is everybody?" I asked one of the shabby Frogs.

"Everyone else is wizdrawn to Beaumont yesterday, *monsieur*," he drawled, pointing westwards.

I checked my map. (Beaumont was thirty bloody miles away.)

"Bloody hell!" I tutted. "You fellows wouldn't have any gin, I suppose?"

"Ah, *non, monsieur.*" (They all frowned and shook their heads ruefully.)

"Just thought I'd ask," I sighed, with a shrug. "Beaumont, you say?"

"*Oui, monsieur.*"

"Any of you fellows heading that way, eh?"

"*Non, monsieur.*"

"Have you any transport?" I enquired.

The Froggy looked left and right. "Erm, *non, monsieur,*" he replied.

"Well, to whom does that bicycle belong?"

"I do not know, *monsieur.*" He shrugged. "It is yours, if you want it, uh?"

The bicycle in question – a rusty, green Minerva – was an absolute piece-of-rubbish boneshaker. (Which was hardly surprising – being of ruddy Belgian manufacture and all.) Nevertheless, I mounted the rickety old thing, bid the Froggies *au revoir*, and trundled-off on my way. The saddle was of appallingly shoddy construction and my entire lower abdominal region was soon aching like buggery. I therefore spent as much time as I could, standing up and pedalling.

The first of the hills which I had to traverse proved to be rather laborious and I was forced to dismount before reaching the top. I then, though, had the pleasure of effortlessly coasting, with the wind rushing through my hair, all the way down the other side.

The brakes had seemed to be reasonably operable when I tested them on level ground. Now though, with my weight on the bike, and travelling downhill at speed, they did very little except make a horrible grinding noise against the rims of the wheels and I continued to gather momentum. I tried to exert some extra pressure on the front calliper using my boot, but the only effect which that had was to make it impossible to steer properly, and I was starting to reach the sort of speed at which any prang might prove to be a jolly nasty one.

It all happened very quickly when it finally did come; one moment I was battling with the brakes and the steering, and the next I was tumbling across the road with the bike clattering-on ahead of me. "Shit and bugger!" I scowled as I blew on the red-raw heels of my palms. I'd bashed-up my bloody left knee too and it hurt like hell. (You know that dull-but-intense, aching throb – deep inside of the joint – when something's twisted that little bit further than it was ever meant to?) "Bastard bloody bike!" I seethed, as I hobbled after it.

The front wheel was a bit buckled, and the handlebar twisted out of alignment, (and I had half a mind to dump the damned shoddy thing there-and-then, to be honest). It was still going to be a good deal quicker than walking though so I climbed back on, resigned to persevering with it. As the hours went by, pines and firs gradually gave way to oak, elm and sycamore, and I came at last to a place where the forest thinned-out and yielded to agriculture; a patchwork of open fields and a little Belgie farming community.

Monsieur Et Madame Gouache

In the north of Belgium (Flanders) is spoken Flemish; a Dutch dialect also known as *Vlaams*. The language of those native to Wallonia, in the south, however (*Walloons*), is a strange French dialect that almost constitutes a separate tongue altogether. (It is pseudo-Froggy, Wallonian-Belgianese, bloody gobbledegook, if you ask me!)

A plump, gnarled, old Belgie fellow was standing in the corner of one of the fields and yelling at a herd of dairy cows. (I sincerely hoped that he was a farmer because, if not, he'd be some kind of cow-pestering bloody lunatic!)

"Greetings, *monsieur*." I smiled amiably as I approached.

"Bonjour," the wizened Walloon replied. "A soldier of zer British you are, oui?"

"Yes, oui." I nodded. "I'm Captain Hugo Poncenby."

"René my name is being," he said. "René Gouache."

"Well, I'm jolly pleased to meet you, Monsieur Gouache," I told him. (Although, whether or not this was *really* so remained to be seen.)

"Grubby you are." He observed. "And a bit smelling."

(*"Huh!"* I thought. *"That's bloody rich, coming from you!"*) "Yes, I became separated from my men when the

Germans attacked Jeuville," I explained, "and was forced to spend last night roughing-it in the woods, I'm afraid."

"Zer dirty Nazi bastards!" he seethed. "But, *monsieur*, you must be not afraid."

"No," I said, shaking my head. "I, erm…" (In the end though, I just couldn't be bothered to try and explain the usage in that context.) "This stupid bloody bicycle is defective and urgently in need of repair," I told him. "Do you, perhaps, have some tools which I might use?"

He nodded. "Best bicycles in zer world, Minerva."

"Hmmm," I said, my eyes narrowing slightly. "Well, this one's suffering from years of neglect; I don't think that it's seen any oil for decades."

"Bring it in," said the shabby old farmer as he opened the gate. "Smartened-up we will soon 'ave 'er, yes?"

"That'd be super." I smiled, wheeling the bike in and leaning it against the fence. "Thanks awfully."

The shabby old farmer started to empty a sack of feed into a nearby trough and we were soon surrounded by mooing, jostling cattle. "Ah, zer girls, I sink, are liking you." He winked, gesturing at the cows.

"Well, that's jolly nice to know." I nodded. "May I assist you with that?"

"Ah, yes, merci." He smiled. "But René you must call me, uh?"

"Very well, René." I nodded as I started to empty-out another sack. (A sharp pain suddenly ripped through my right shoulder and I dropped the sack of feed into the trough.) "Ooh, bugger!" I winced.

"Monsieur, 'urt you are!" the old Belgie exclaimed. "Shot you 'ave been, no?"

"Mm, it's just a little nick really," I said, cradling my shoulder, "but it's rendered the old arm a bit stiff."

Farmer Gouache finished emptying out the feed and tucked the empty sacks under his arm. "Come, mon amis," he beckoned. "Zese wounds my wife will tend to."

The old Belgie seemed like a pleasant enough fellow. (Why he found it so difficult to construct an easily intelligible sentence I put down to his being a rustic, rural type – some *British* yokels can be just as babbling and abstruse you know!) He stuffed the empty feed sacks into a large, rusty, metal bin outside the farmhouse and invited me inside to meet his wife.

"Marguerite, mon cherie, Yugo ziss young man's name is being," he told the old girl. "A British soldier he is and by zer dirty 'orrible bloody Germans 'as been shot."

"Very pleased to meet you madam," I smiled.

"Mon Dieu!" She winced. "At ziss shoulder I will look, and zen at zat 'ead also. You are sitting, please."

"Pretty bloody 'ot she is, *non*?" René winked as the old bird went to fetch bandages, lint and iodine.

"Hot?" I shrugged, shaking my head.

"Sexy."

"Oh, erm…Mmmm." I nodded. (Were she about 150 years younger, perhaps!)

"A little bit rubbish your English girls are, *n'est pas*?"

"Oh, no-no-no!" I frowned. "No, they're very lovely indeed on the whole."

"Well, about my Marguerite, get no ideas, *monsieur*; you British types I know very well!"

"Good Lord!" I gasped. "You've no worries there, I can assure you."

"Why?" He frowned.

"Well." I shrugged. "I mean – as unquestionably fair as Madame Gouache is – my *mother* is younger than she!"

"Oh?" said René, raising a bushy eyebrow. "A pretty lady your moser is, oui?"

(*'Steady-on, you libidinous old bugger!'* I thought.) "She's a wonderful woman." I nodded.

I considered whether or not Father would have had me tear the bumpkin's arms and legs off for such impertinence. (On reflection though I suspected that, during his lifetime, the major had probably seen more than enough slaughtered Belgies for the both of us.)

Madame Gouache very gently (and deftly) replaced the dressing on my shoulder but the lump on my head and the gash on my cheek required only a little clean-up and so she agreed to leave them uncovered. I then followed the old boy back outside to a little shed which served as his workshop and (under his constant and unnecessary supervision); I soon had the crappy old bike in rather better working order.

"Hungry you are, Yugo?" he asked.

"Why, yes." I nodded. "Now that you mention it, I *am* a little peckish as a matter of fact."

"Speaking very strangely you are!" He laughed.

"Mm. Likewise, eh?" I nodded, smiling broadly.

"Come," he said. "Time to eat it is."

The Belgies like three meals a day: a light brekkie, a modest lunch, and a really quite substantial dinner. It has been said that Belgie food is served in Jerry quantity but is, in quality, the equal of Froggy cuisine. (Which, frankly, doesn't take *much* doing, does it?)

"*Tarines*?" Madame Gouache smiled.

"Erm, not as far as I know." I shrugged.

Tarines though, turned-out to be nothing more sinister or afflictive than some rustic, farmhouse bread, served on a cutting board, with some chunky pâté. (Which I discovered, to my delight, was made with wild boar; and was absolutely bloody delicious!)

"*Gueuze*?" asked the old boy.

"Mm." I smiled weakly. "Again, I'm not *entirely* certain actually."

I subsequently learned from René that gueuze is a Belgian beer, made from a one to two-year-old Lambic, blended with a two- to three-year-old, and then re-fermented; it has a dry, acidic, cidery taste and is sometimes known, due to its carbonation, as 'Brussels Champagne'. It was really a *very* good complement to the pâté.

"And now," said Marguerite "*Anguilles au vert*."

(*'Hmmm. Now,* vert *is green, isn't it?'* I mused. '*Then what on earth is* anguilles*? There's an island in the Caribbean called Anguilla; they export a lot of lobster; lobsters are of the order Decapodia… Ah, now, the order of fish known as Anguilliformes are…?'*)

"Oh, it's eel!" I nodded. "Eel in green, eh?"

Anguilles au vert is eel in a green sauce made of mixed herbs like chervil and parsley. Madame Gouache served it with fries and, whilst reasonably palatable, it was the strangest-looking fish and chips that I'd ever seen in my life! (And mayonnaise with chips is just *wrong*!)

To round off the meal, Marguerite served a magnificent Brussels waffle, stuffed with fresh fruit, drizzled with syrup and fresh cream, and dusted with icing sugar. (I'm afraid that I have to give the Belgies that one; the waffle.)

"On zer wireless." Marguerite frowned. "Zer man was saying zat, over Liège and Namur, zer Nazi flag is now flying."

"Strewth!" I tutted, shaking my head.

"Wiz zer dirty, 'orrible bastards I sink Belgium will soon be overrun." René scowled. (Just how ghastly it must be to reside in a country which borders with Germany one can scarcely imagine.)

"I say, René, do you think it would be all right if I tuned the wireless to the old BBC presently, for a bit of a listen?"

"Fine ziss will be I sink." He nodded. "Marguerite, mon cherie, to zer BBC Yugo wishes to listen."

"Oh, but yes, of course." She smiled as she cleared the table.

I twirled the wireless dial until a crackly English voice could be heard. The news was most disheartening. Guderian's panzers had found a way through the Ardennes; they had crossed the Meuse at Sedan, completely flanking the Maginot Line, and were now pouring into France in their bloody thousands. More sodding tanks were reportedly crossing at Dinant, too.

"My God, it's all sounding a bit grim." I frowned. "Dinant has fallen and the Jerries have captured the bridge at Sedan."

"Bloody Frenchies!" he sneered "Pah!"

I got the distinct impression that there was little love lost between this particular Belgie and his Froggy neighbours. (Personally, I still can't tell the two shabby nationalities apart.)

"Come!" the portly old farmer suddenly demanded. "Wiz me, you will drink zer gin, oui?"

"Gin?" I exclaimed. "Oh, smashing! Abso-bloody-lutely! Thanks awfully."

Each of us armed with his pipe and tobacco, René and I retired to the sitting room and laid-into his Dutch gin. (I was soon so squiffy that I damned nearly started to tell Monsieur Gouache the one about *Fake Belgium*!) The shoddy, Swiss-style cuckoo clock, hanging on the wall, indicated that it was 23:55.

"Well, René," I said at last. "I cannot thank you and Marguerite enough for your splendid gerenosity and warm hostipality, but I'm afraid that I musht get back to my platoon, and so I shall have to bid you farewell and take my leave."

"No." He frowned. "Not one shingle word of ziss did I undershtand."

"Why, I musht now go," I slurred, "And rejoin my men!"

"Ha!" He chuckled. "Midnight it will be soon, Yugo, and very pissed you are! Stay 'ere and leave in zer morning you will, yes?"

"Well, I mean, only if you're quite sure." I shrugged. "I *am* a teensy bit tiddly for cycling, I suppose."

"Zer spare bedroom, for you, I 'ave made ready." Marguerite smiled.

"Oh, that's so very good of you." I nodded. "Thank you very much. Merci beaucoup."

The room in question may have been a little shabby but the bed was clean and comfortable at least, and in no time at all I was away in the land of Nod.

I awoke during the night and, at first, I thought that I could hear distant artillery shells. I then concluded that the knocking noise must be due to shoddy Wallonian plumbing. (I soon realised, however, that it was the headboard in the bedroom next door, banging against the wall as the prurient old Belgie couple went at it.)

"Ugh!" I grimaced.

I also couldn't help a little chuckle though, and only hoped that I still had the inclination and energy by the time that I reached that age. (Which, in case anybody was wondering, I absolutely do!)

My assumption that it would all be over very quickly proved to be wishful thinking and eventually it got so ridiculous that I had to shift the bed away from the wall and bury my head beneath the pillow in order to get back to sleep.

Very early the next morning (after some waffles, strong coffee, and a pipe or two), René prepared himself for another day on the farm and I prepared myself for another day in the bloody saddle.

"I cannot thank you both enough," I told the Gouaches. "*Merci, mes amis*."

"Very welcome you are." René smiled, grabbing me in an embrace.

"To you, good luck, Yugo," said Marguerite. "Stay alive, yes?"

"I shall certainly endeavour to do so." I winked, placing a kiss on each of her wrinkled cheeks.

The Belgies had gone up in my estimation (marginally at least); René and Marguerite Gouache were good, decent people – even if they *did* insist on putting mayonnaise on their ruddy chips.

Having been gifted with fresh water and a drop of gin for the old hip flask, a couple of wild boar sausages, and a large, home-baked *couque* (a biscuit of Dinantian origin), I set-off once again. Conditions were favourable; the sky overhead was clear and blue with only a few smudges of white cloud here and there.

I arrived in Beaumont around midday but was more than a little peeved to be told that the platoon had been ordered to withdraw to Valenciennes and had left hours ago. (The latest on the Jerry advance was bloody depressing too.) Again, there seemed to be no other transport available and so I was left with no choice but to continue my journey on the stupid bloody bike. I'd soon crossed into France though and, after a time, the landscape began to slope-away onto broad lowlands. The sun was still shining brightly in the blue sky, and there was no hint of bad weather. (France, I think we have established, is an utterly ghastly and awful place; due to it being predominantly populated by stupid, rancid, cowardly Froggies.)

After a time, I began to feel rather peckish so I pulled over to the side of the road and rummaged through my pack for the Belgie boar sausages and the *couque*. The sausages were first class; succulent, meaty and delicious. I devoured them voraciously, scoffed the biscuit for afters, and then indulged in a tot of gin and a quick draw on the old pipe.

Michelle Dégoûtante

Subsequent to my little picnic lunchbreak I was trundling along a narrow lane, wending my merry way towards a Froggy village called Sâuver, when there came a woman's cry and I stopped and dismounted. As I listened, I heard more voices; male; German; laughing. I left the bike, whipped out my revolver, and crept forward, through the bushes.

I soon spotted two filthy Jerry bounders, in an adjacent road, manhandling a young French female (brunette, early twenties, *very* pretty; in a little floral-patterned summer dress and pink cardigan). The girl suddenly lashed-out at her tormentors and made a run for it and I couldn't believe my eyes when one of the cads slipped the rifle from his shoulder and took aim at the fleeing filly.

"No you bloody don't!" I scowled. ("Bang!" went my .38. "Bang! Bang!")

I went to check that both of the rotters were dead and the poor girl fell, sobbing, into my arms.

"*Oh, mon Dieu!*" She cried. "*Merci, monsieur.*"

"There, there," I said, "you're all right now, my dear."

"You are English?" she asked, gazing up at me with big, dark, teary eyes.

"Hugo Poncenby, of the British Expeditionary Force." I smiled.

"Zer Nazis, are zey…?"

"Dead?" I said. "Yes, their bullying, fascist days are over."

"Oh, Monsieur Poncenby, you 'ave saved me!"

"Call me Hugo." I winked.

"I am Michelle." She smiled. "Michelle Dégoûtant."

"Well, I'm most very pleased to meet you, Michelle," I told her. (*'Most* very *pleased indeed!'*)

The pretty, young Frenchie related that she was returning home from her grandmother's, in Préseau, when she was waylaid and accosted by the pair of dirty, rotten Nazis.

"You've had a nasty shock, my dear," I said. "Have some gin."

"Oh, no sank you," she replied, shaking her pretty head. "I will be all right."

"Well, neither of us had better hang around here," I told her, taking a quick swig myself. "Perhaps you had better return to your grandmother's? I can take you there; as long as you don't mind riding two-up."

I escorted the young lady to the spot where I'd left the bike, retrieved it from the undergrowth, and wheeled it back onto the road.

"I shall sit on zer front, oui?" she said. "On zer…*steering?*"

"On the handlebar?" I frowned. "Are you sure?"

"Zer saddle looks very uncomfortable," she grimaced.

"Yes," I sighed, "it is rather."

I took another nice glug of gin as I watched her perch her firm, rounded buttocks on the handlebar.

"Ready?" I asked, slipping the flask back into my pocket.

"Oui." She nodded. "I am ready."

"Off we go then."

(Of course, one would never *purposely* take advantage of such a situation in order to peek down the front of a young lady's blouse and ogle her smooth, firm, and well-formed breasts. It just happened that, every time I glanced down, there they were jiggling-about with every bump in the *very* uneven road.) With the general semi-on, and dribbling down my leg, we eventually arrived in Préseau and Michelle directed me to the little farmstead where her grandmother resided.

"It is late, Yugo," she said, gently lowering herself from the bike. "You must be very tired. You are welcome stay 'ere for zer night."

"Well, I, er, wouldn't want to impose," I told her, draining my hip flask. "It *is* rather late though, eh?"

"You can sleep in zer barn," she said. "Zer 'ay is nice and soft and warm."

"Ah, yes, of course, the *barn*." I smiled weakly. "Right-ho. Thanks."

Whilst I got myself settled in the sodding barn, Michelle went to round up a bit of supper and soon returned with bread, butter, jam, apples, wine, and a wedge of Brie.

"Oh, you sweet thing!" I exclaimed. "Thank you *so* much, my dear."

"Zer bread is freshly baked," she said, seating herself next to me. "It is nice and soft and warm."

The fresh bread, smothered in butter and jam, was absolutely first class. The apples were crisp and sweet, and the wine passable. (I couldn't help wondering, though, why these continental types are incapable of making *proper* cheese.)

"I'm sorry zat zere was not more," she sighed.

"Not at all," I replied. "That was as splendid a supper as I have ever had."

"Shall I bring some more wine?" she asked as she collected-up the supper things onto the tray.

"You wouldn't happen to have anything a bit stronger, would you?" I asked her. "A drop of gin, perhaps?"

"No, I'm sorry, zere is no gin," she replied, shaking her head. "But my grand-mère 'as some *eau-de-vie*."

"Ugh!" I grimaced. "I'm not sure that I want to drink your granny's Odour-vee, actually."

"I will bring some." She laughed. "You can try a little, yes?"

"Well, all right then," I said, "why not, eh? I'll give it a little go."

Try as I might, I was unable to tear my gaze away from Michelle's lovely French buttocks, as she sauntered back up to the house with the tray. She soon returned, carrying a bottle of yellowish stuff; it looked like a pale, single-malt whisky but tasted, to my palate, not unlike brandy. (It was strong liquor at least!)

"I say, in lieu of gin, that's not at all bad," I declared. "Won't you join me, my dear?"

"No." She smiled. "I will just 'ave some wine, I sink. Tell me about zer fighting in Wallonia, Yugo. Was it scary and 'orrible?" (As I am often wont to do, I tried to play-down the seriousness of the situation as I related the events of the previous couple of days to the pretty, young Frenchie. She was, nevertheless, lapping-up every single word.) "My, but you are *so* brave," she cooed. "To endure such 'ell, you must be zer superman!"

"No, no," I said. "It's really all in a day's work for a soldier in the *British* Army."

"Is it true zat zer Nazis nailed a priest to zer door of 'is church and raped all of zer nuns?"

"Well, I'm not sure about that, my dear." I frowned, "but I *do* know that they are vile, rotten swine who need some bloody sense beaten into them."

"But, 'ow will zat 'appen now, Yugo?" she sighed. "Wiz zeir tanks and zeir big guns; zey seem unstoppable."

"No," I said, shaking my head. "They're a determined bunch of bounders, I'll grant you, but they can *never* win this war with the rotten values which they've been force-fed. No, you mark my words; those vile Nazis will get what's coming to them if *I* have anything to do with it!"

Michelle's pupils dilated as she gazed into my eyes. "Would you like me to stay wiz you for a while?" she whispered. "I am nice and soft and warm." (*'Hello!'*)

We reclined in the hay and I comforted her for a bit, paused for a quick puff on the old briar and a swig of eau-de-vie, and then comforted her again before sinking into blissful sleep. (As accommodating as Michelle was, I wondered what French women found so damned difficult about getting a razor and shaving their ruddy armpits!)

At sunrise the next morning I was awoken by a broom. It was wielded by a wrinkled old Froggy crone, who used it to deliver a series of stinging blows whilst ranting some drawling French nonsense at me.

"I've no idea what you're saying, you hideous crone!" I scowled, trying to protect my more vulnerable parts. (More

156

inane Froggy babbling.) "I told you, I haven't a clue what you're waffling on about, you rancid old battle-axe! Where is Michelle?"

The mention of the girl's name sent the old bag into a bloody frenzy and she again set-about me with the damned broom.

"Pack it in with that bloody thing!" I growled, grabbing hold of the broom head.

The old cow babbled more nonsense but I did manage to pick-out one crucial thing: *'Les Nazis'*.

Michelle arrived moments later and filled-in the gaps for me; Jerry was on his bloody way into Préseau!

"Take zese," she said, handing me a couple of bottles of eau-de-vie. "For you and your brave men."

I tucked them into the empty ammo pouches on my webbing and took her in my arms. "I cannot thank you enough for your kindness," I told her, planting a big kiss on her rosy French lips.

"Oy! Roast beef!" The old bag glared, bashing me with the broom.

I thanked Michelle once again, scowled at her rancid grandmother, and then leapt on the bike and scarpered.

Just north of Préseau, near a place called Saultain, was a bridge over the river Sambre. Valenciennes was only a little further; the town was in utter bloody chaos and disarray but I spotted a familiar face amidst all the confusion.

"Farringdon, old boy!" I called out.

"Poncenby?" he exclaimed. "Bloody hell, Hugo! Your chaps said that you were dead!"

"Huh!" I sniffed. "The silly buggers ought to know me better than that!"

"Nice bike," Farringdon smirked, nodding at the old Minerva.

"It's a rickety piece of Belgie crap!" I frowned. "But *needs must*, Charles; it got me here, at least."

"Well it's frightfully good to see you; alive and all."

"You too." I winked. "When and where did you see my lads then?"

"This morning," he replied. "Colonel Brompton ordered your chaps to report to him in Lille. The whole Picardy region is swarming with Jerry's armoured infantry so everybody's heading north. We're moving out shortly too. Ditch the bike and hop on board, eh?"

I was only too glad to dump the bloody stupid Minerva bike and clamber aboard Farringdon's truck. A couple of minutes later I was on my way to Lille.

"How's the old, erm…posterior?" I discreetly enquired of Farringdon.

"Do you know what? They're far from cured," he replied, "but that plantain juice thing really does seem to have made a difference."

"Good." I nodded. "Glad to hear it, old boy. I may yet have cause to resort to it myself."

We soon arrived in Lille and I spied a familiar-looking pair of Commer Q4s. There my lads were; every one of them with a face like a smacked arse. Farringdon pulled-up nearby.

"You there?" I yelled. "That man!"

"Fuck me!" Manning gasped.

"I'd rather not, thank you." I frowned, climbing down from the truck.

"Sir!!!" Tucker exclaimed. "Bugger me!"

"Good God!" I scowled. "What the hell is wrong with you lot? A couple of days without me, and you're all pleading to be shafted up the backside! Have you been drinking rum?"

"No, sir, we've 'ad nothin' but char since yesterday, when the Con-yack ran out," Manning said glumly. "I don't s'pose you came across any gin did you, sir?"

"No, I'm afraid not," I sighed, opening one of my ammo pouches. "I do have *this* though; it's called 'Odour-vee'. It's not gin but it *is* 80% proof."

"We thought you'd copped-it when the gin palace went up, sir," said Hawkins.

"Don't be daft," I grinned. "Jerry will have to try a lot bloody harder than that if he wants to finish *me* off!" (I didn't believe this for a moment, of course; I had just been damned lucky, that was all.)

Manning distributed eau-de-vie amongst the chaps.

"Ooh, it tastes a bit weird, sir." Ferguson frowned.

"Not unpleasant-weird though, eh?"

"Nah." He shrugged. "It's not 'orrible."

"Whoo-hoo! It's got a kick, right enough!" Davenport exclaimed. "What did you say it was called, sir?"

"Odour-vee."

"Well, it might not be gin, sir." He smiled. "But it's not bad."

I turned to Manning. "Sergeant?"

"Mm." Manning nodded. "Yeah, it's all right, sir."

(I quietly breathed a sigh of relief.)

"Oh, well done, sir!" Tucker suddenly blubbered. "What an absolute legend you are! In years t'come, drunken soldiers will sit-around and sing songs about you, sir!"

159

"All right now, steady-on, Tubbs!" I told him sternly. "Drink up your Odour-vee and you'll be fine, lad."

The chaps would, of course, much rather have had a drop of gin, but, once they were all full of eau-de-vie, they were right back on form. "Hurrah!" they cheered.

The R-Word

Despite a few minor short-comings, the chaps in my platoon really *were* a sterling bunch and I still hold the firm belief that, had our continental comrades been endowed with a tad more courage, then Hitler's little Nazi tour of Europe might have been nipped-in-the-bud at that time. (This is merely my own assertion though, of course, and many of those self-proclaimed, so-called 'historians' will doubtless be unlikely to concur.) Anyway, the next day brought some very bad news indeed.

"I've just received a rather disturbing message," I told the lads gravely. "It indicated that Jerry has captured Abbeville and is starting to work his way up the coast towards Calais. If he should make it that far, then he will have us all-but surrounded."

"My God, how can that *be*, sir?" Manning scowled.

"Well," I sighed. "I rather fear that most of the Frenchies have lost the will to fight you know."

"Lost the will to fight, sir?" He shrugged. "What d'you mean?"

"Acute bottle fatigue," I told him. "It happens all-too-easily with these limp-wristed Europeans; in 1870, Bismarck manoeuvred Napoleon the Third – *Louis-Napoleon* – into

161

starting the Franco-Prussian War and, by May the following year, the Frogs had gone completely belly up; they surrendered at Sedan, funnily enough. With the signing of the Treaty of Frankfurt, Prussia won the provinces of Alsace and Lorraine – and a sizeable indemnity too. The Frenchies' Second Republic then collapsed, establishing a unified Germany as the leading power in Europe – which is, of course, the very same damned German empire which we then had to help all of these knock-kneed pansies to put down during the last war."

"I can understand a bit of a flap in the face of a good old onslaught, sir," said Tucker, "and even a nasty, whiffy mess in the old undies, but how can a chap lose his bottle altogether?"

"I know that it's very hard for a British soldier to comprehend." I nodded. "But you have to remember that all of these continental types are born with very spindly and insubstantial backbones to start with – it's a wonder that most of them are even able to stand upright. You take a chap like that and show him a couple of decent battles, and you've got yourself one dedicated white flag-waver!"

"They're really *that* gutless, sir?" asked Manning.

"Oh yes," I replied, with a nod, "the Frenchies even have an elite surrender squad you know."

"A *what*?"

"Mm. They employ a wide range of pusillanimous tactics: crying, hiding, running away, pant-shitting, fainting, pleading for mercy…"

"Oh, sir." He chuckled. "You 'ad me goin' for a second!"

"No, I'm serious, lad. They can run-up a white flag in the blink of an eye."

"A crack surrender squad, eh?"

"Mm-hm." I nodded. "They do these special arm-raising exercises," (I put my hands in the air.)

"Arm-raising, yeah?" Manning laughed.

"Oh yes." I winked. "*Very* good at the old arm-raising they are. Of course, your average Jerry is every bit as cowardly and spineless as your Frog, you know. Herr Hitler is able to maintain his grip on power, and leadership of the Nazi party itself, only *because* terror is so easily induced in such invertebrate maggots. That's what their bloody blitzkrieg tactics are all about."

Hawkins screwed-up his nose and I knew roughly what was coming next: "What's Prick's-League tactics then, sir?"

"*Blitz-krieg*," I tutted. "It means 'lightning-war' and equates to wholesale, Viking-style pillage; merciless marauding and maiming, relentless rampaging, rape and robbery!" (Hm. I *am* somewhat given to inadvertent alliteration, aren't I? I shall have to watch-out for that.)

"Strewth!" Hawk-eye gasped. "The rotten bastards!"

"Mm." I nodded. "Didn't I tell you that they were vile bloody swine?"

The Jerry offensive seemed to stall somewhat over the next few days. It was not to be for long, but it at least afforded us a chance to dig-in, round up some ammo and supplies, and get some defences in place. On May the 26th, however, the inconceivable came to pass and the BEF was ordered to…to…*retreat*!

"Retreat?" I glared. "I didn't come all the bloody way over here to turn-tail and run away. We are Halberdiers – we do not *do* the R-word!"

"They're sending ships to evacuate us from Dunkirk," said Farringdon. "It's the only bloody port still left open to us."

"I don't bloody believe it! How can this be happening?" I scowled. "It's a war of movement, all right; but in the wrong sodding direction."

"Incoming!" Somebody yelled and everybody hit the deck. There was a sudden, loud BANG! And flaming bits of Gertrude were dispersed (in a most dramatic and lethal manner) over a large area.

"Take cover!" I yelled as another 88 mm round came whooshing-in and exploded nearby. "Everyone find some bloody cover!"

The barrage was not sustained though, and seemed to me to be little more than a few mindless pot-shots. (It might be a very different story once Jerry had zeroed-in on us however; the next bombardment, if and when it came, would likely be a good deal more punishing.)

"Hinckley's down, sir," said Manning, pointing.

"Hinckley?" I called out, breaking cover and running to him.

"Nicholas!" He spluttered. (He'd taken some shrapnel to the face and chest.)

"What?"

"I jus' goddit, sir!" he coughed. "They called her *knickerless*…huh-huh…"

"Oh, Hinckley…" I sighed. (I was glad that the thick Brummie had finally got it; but *so* saddened that he'd also *got it*.) A medic arrived within moments, with dressings and morphine at the ready, but I shook my head at him and then went to check on the rest of the chaps.

"We lost Trubshaw and Stainer as well, sir," Manning reported. "And the Odour-vee went up with Gertie, sir; it's all...it's *gone*."

"No, I don't believe it!" I growled. "My bloody pipe and tobacco were in there too!"

"What'll we do, sir?"

Without alcohol or tobacco, there seemed to be no point in staying (and little point to anything else for that matter) and so, very reluctantly, I ordered everybody onto our one remaining truck and we headed for Dunkirk, along with what was left of Captain Farringdon's company.

"It's about forty miles, from here to Dunkirk," I told Manning as we trundled along. "Barring any unforeseen circumstances, we have plenty of fuel for the journey and a bit left over."

"Good." He nodded. "That's good, sir."

"Yes, so I'm going to drop you chaps there and take Bertha to Calais."

"You what, sir?" he gasped.

"Listen," I said, "the only reason that Dunkirk is still open to us is that some bloody brave chaps have given their all – and then some more – in defence of Calais."

"Well, yeah, sir, but..."

"No, no buts," I told him. "There are British soldiers in peril!"

Within the hour, we had arrived at the outskirts of Dunkirk and what a bloody extraordinary sight it was; the roads were strewn with abandoned vehicles and pieces of smashed and twisted equipment lay scattered everywhere.

"See if you can round up some grog, eh?" I told Manning as we pulled-up. "I don't care what it is – I'd drink bloody schnapps right now."

"Ooh, Christ! No need for *that*, sir." He frowned, rummaging in his pocket and producing a little 2 oz. hip flask. "Here."

"Is that...*alcohol*, Sergeant?" I gasped.

"I saved-up a couple of my rations, back when we 'ad the Dutch gin, sir." He nodded. "For emergencies, like."

"Good Lord!" I exclaimed. "You've had gin on you this whole time?"

"Well, I was hoping that the situation wouldn't arise, sir."

"But I can't possibly deprive you of it, lad."

"Oh, it was never meant for *me*, sir." He shrugged.

"No?"

"No, it's for you, sir. It was in case of, well...summink like *this*."

"Oh God, I'm genuinely bloody touched, lad!" I said. "You saved *your* gin rations up for *me*?"

"Well, yeah," he replied. "We'd be right up the bloody creek without you, sir."

(I took a little sip of the old Dutch gin and felt its restorative powers begin to permeate my body, spreading to every remote corner of my being, and all angst and fatigue was soon washed away.)

"I think that we ought to pool the rest of our resources," I told him. "Collect-up everybody's cigarettes and tobacco – smoking is now subject to rationing."

"Yep, right-ho, sir." He nodded.

I dismounted and went to answer the call of nature and it felt like I was pissing hot sand. "Argh!" I gasped. "What the hell…?" (What a bloody lousy time to get a urinary tract infection, eh? Mm…)

Wearing a deeply furrowed brow, and waving his right hand, Captain Farringdon came striding over to the truck. "I've just heard your lads waffling some nonsense about you going to Calais, Hugo?" He frowned.

"Yes, that's right." I nodded. "I know it sounds a bit mad, Charles, but…"

"A bit mad?" he gasped. "It's bloody insane! You mustn't go, old boy."

"Conscience will not allow me to leave without attempting to get more chaps out," I told him. "It's only a few miles down the road."

"Don't go, sir!" Hawk-eye pleaded forlornly.

"Don't you worry about me, my lad." I laughed. "I'm Captain H. J. bloody Poncenby, I am!"

"At least let me come too then, sir," said Manning.

"No," I sighed, "you'd be taking-up some other fellow's place."

"I'll come back on the roof." He shrugged.

"If there's any space on the roof, the same thing applies," I told him. "Anyway, I need you here to maintain discipline."

"All right, sir. We'll be right here."

(I hereby confess that, despite all of the morale-boosting bravado, my arse was twitching madly; I was gravely concerned and couldn't see how on earth I was going to make it to Calais, and back again, without drawing fire somewhere. If there was even the slim chance of pulling it off though, I would be unfit to call myself an Englishman if I did not at least bloody-well try!)

167

Operation Fish Market

A great swathe of thick, charcoal-grey cloud hung in the sky to the east and, as I pulled-out, there came a faraway rumble of thunder. Either side of the road a long, snaking line of wounded and forlorn-looking chaps were making their dejected way eastwards along the Boulevard de Gravedines. Calais itself was a bloody disaster area; Jerry was pounding the city, utterly mercilessly, with his big guns. What was left of the British contingent of the defensive rear-guard had pulled-back and retreated to the north-east. As politely as possible, I urged them to most hastily embark.

"Oy! You lot!" I cried. "Get in the bloody truck!"

"Sir?" said a bemused-looking sergeant. "Are you evacuating us, sir?"

"Yes, I sodding-well am! Get your lads, and as many of the Frenchies as you can, in the back!"

"Oh, thank Christ! Come on, chaps; we're getting out of here!"

"Hurrah!" his lads cheered.

At first, I couldn't place the Froggy voice: "*Mon Dieu!*" it exclaimed. "Capitaine Poncenby?"

It was Dauphinois; the flaming French fauchardier fellow. (There's that alliteration again!)

"Captain Dolphin-wah!" I gasped. "Well, bugger me sideways! What the bloody hell are *you* doing here?"

A series of shocking and woeful pastings had apparently led to the surviving Frenchies fleeing for their lives. "We 'ad to retreat to Abbeville," Dauphinois explained, "and, since zen, we 'ave been fighting zer losing battles all zer way up zer bloody coast!"

Previously, Dauphinois's men had been blood-spattered, tired and dispirited. Now, most of them were horribly wounded, utterly exhausted, and they all looked thoroughly traumatised.

"Quick then, jump aboard, old chap," I beckoned with a wave of my thumb.

"But, *monsieur*, I cannot leave my men!" he said, shaking his head.

"Well look, I'm pretty bloody full-up and I have to go," I told him. "You and your chaps wait here though; I *will* be back."

"We will wait 'ere, *monsieur*." He nodded. "We 'ave, anyway, nowhere else to go."

On the way through Gravedines the truck caught the attention of a lone, opportunistic, Stuka dive-bomber; it fell, screaming, into a steep dive, released its payload, and explosions erupted all around.

"Jesus Christ!" I gasped, swerving this way and that.

Thankfully though, we took no direct hits; the Stuka buggered-off elsewhere, and we lurched onwards.

"Strewth! That was nice drivin', sir," said the sergeant.

"Yes, it wasn't bad, was it?" I smiled. "What's your name, Sergeant?"

"Sargent, sir."

I shot him a sideways look. "Sergeant Sargent?" I grinned.

"Yeah." He nodded. "But at least it's less confusing than when I was *Corporal* Sargent, sir."

"Mm. Somewhere in there, there *must* be a witticism that you haven't already heard."

"I've heard most of 'em, sir."

There was a sudden, loud "BANG!" and the truck began to shudder violently. (In the back, someone's arse went "Pffrrt!")

"Damn!" I growled.

"Are we hit, sir?" asked Sargent.

"No," I replied. "I think that was another suspension spring going."

"Another one?" he gasped.

"*Nil desperandum*, eh?" I tutted. "That's the least of our bloody worries!"

I arrived back at the RV and the grateful evacuees disembarked.

"Boothroyd's already buggered-off home," said Farringdon. "I'm afraid that I've been ordered to pull my lads out immediately. I'll get all of these chaps down to the port, eh?"

"Yep, right-ho, old boy." I nodded. "We'll be following right behind."

I nipped out of sight for a pee and it felt very much like I was passing broken glass. "Oh, Jesus!" I gasped, gripping onto the truck, my knees trembling. ("Pffrrt!" my backside trumpeted.)

"All right, sir?" asked Manning.

"Yep, fine," I winced as I zipped-up my fly. "What's the latest?"

"It sounds pretty grim I'm afraid, sir." He frowned. "The bloody Luftwaffe are bombing the beaches, and the ships out at sea; they've already sunk a couple of destroyers."

"The rotten, filthy bastards!" I scowled. "Corporal Davenport, find me some petrol, lad."

"Christ, you're *never* goin' back to Calais, sir?" Manning gasped.

"I most certainly am," I replied. (I suddenly spotted a .50-calibre Browning heavy machine gun.) "Bring me that fifty and find some bloody ammo for it!"

I yanked the .303 from its mount, hurled it to the side of the road, and then hoisted the .50 into its place.

"You've done more than enough already, sir," said Manning, handing me an ammo belt. "You don't *have* to go back."

"Yes, lad, I do," I told him. "There are some Frenchies there who have made a lot of sacrifices holding-back the Hun; I think that even the courage of despair has earned them the chance to evacuate, don't you?"

"Maybe, sir." He sighed. "But this truck's *never* gonna make it there and back again!"

"Right." I tutted. "*When* I return, you will apologise to Bertha for your lack of faith in her, understood?"

"I'll pucker-up and kiss her bloody rusty exhaust, sir!"

I noticed that Tucker was trembling uncontrollably.

"Are you all right there, Tubbs?" I asked.

"Yeah, I feel fine, sir," he assured me. "I just can't seem to stop the shakes."

"Any dizziness or nausea?"

"A bit, sir." He grinned. "But only 'cos of Hawk-eye's rotten arse."

"Oh, I didn't, did I?" Hawkins frowned, trying to crane his neck around to inspect the seat of his britches.

"No." Tubby chuckled. "Not this time, mate."

"I think that you and the other chaps ought to get yourselves out of here, you know," I told Manning.

"But I can't leave without you, sir," he exclaimed. "It wouldn't be right."

"Look at these chaps," I said. "They've fought fearlessly and effectively, and they despise what's going on every bit as much as you and I, but they're exhausted and most of them require further medical attention. Now, I *know* these lads and they won't leave without me unless they're bloody-well escorted onto a boat."

"That's easy, sir." He shrugged. "Corporal Davenport!"

"Sarge?"

"Get the remaining platoon members down to the beach, and onto a boat, right away," Manning told him.

"Yes, sir." Davenport nodded.

"There you are sir." Manning winked. "Sorted."

"All right." I tutted, sighing deeply. "Here."

I handed him back the little hip flask and he shook it.

"There's still some in there, sir."

"Look after it for me, eh? I don't want anything to happen to it – I shall probably be bloody-well needing it by the time that I get back!"

I knew that my chances of getting there and back in one piece were slim to none at all. Nevertheless, I started-up the spluttering engine and put the truck into gear; as I eased off the clutch and released the hand brake, my right foot gently pushed down on the accelerator and the decrepit Commer slowly began to heave herself forwards.

My mind was racing as I approached Calais; there were sporadic flashes of bright orange and tall plumes of thick, black smoke were rising over the port area. Dauphinois and his rag-tag band of shabby Froggies were cowering behind one of the only buildings which still stood intact.

"Come on then, you bloody Frogs!" I yelled. "I am leaving immediately and I am *definitely* not bloody-well coming back!"

It was only those hapless Frenchies who were already deceased that declined; the rest of them clambered aboard. (What remained of poor old Bertha's suspension heaved under the weight as we pulled out.)

We made it as far as Gravedines before we ran into trouble.

"Messerschmitt, *monsieur*!" Dauphinois gasped.

I could see the bugger in the rear-view mirror and noted the muzzle-flashes as he opened-fire on us.

"Here, take the wheel," I said. "Can you drive?"

"*Oui, monsieur*." He nodded.

"Good; drive then!" I told him as I clambered up to man the .50-cal.

I got the 109 in my sights and let-rip: "Duh-duh-duh-duh-duh!" the heavy machine gun thudded. "Duh-duh-duh-duh-duh-duh-duh!" I watched as the tracer rounds found their mark, and half-inch bullets started to rip into the Messerschmitt as I continued to unload. Fire erupted inside the cockpit and the plane promptly dropped from the sky, billowing thick, black smoke, and slammed into the ground with a thunderous BOOM!

"*Mon Dieu!*" one of the other Frogs gasped as I climbed back into the driver's seat. "*Formidable, monsieur!*"

173

"We are on fire, *monsieur!*" Dauphinois cried.

"So what?" I shrugged, looking in the wing mirror.

"Erm…" He frowned. "We are on *fire!*"

"It's only a tyre," I told him. "The petrol tank's virtually empty and we're nearly there now anyway."

My face contorted into a deep grimace and I looked over at Dauphinois.

"Eurgh! *Sacre bleu!*" he suddenly exclaimed. "What zer 'ell is zat 'orrible stink?"

"Ugh!" one of his men groaned. "I 'ave made a nasty toilet inside of my pantaloons, mon capitaine!"

"*Mon Dieu!*" Dauphinois scowled.

"I too 'ave a very bad mess inside of my underwear," another of them confessed.

"And me also," added a third.

The roads into Dunkirk were so littered with abandoned vehicles and discarded bits of equipment that they soon became completely impassable and we were forced to ditch Bertha and continue on foot. (The poor old Commer Q4 was in a pitiful state; were she a horse, I would've put a bloody bullet in her head!) She'd got us there though, and another thirty or forty chaps – who would otherwise have been captured or killed – had been saved.

"Oh, *monsieur*, you 'ave saved us!" one of the bashed-up old Froggies sobbed. "I shall never forget you, sir!"

"Yes, well, let's keep it moving, eh?" I frowned. "Straight-on, down the road." (We'd all been through a lot of unpleasantness but I *do* despise chaps blubbering like that!)

The air was filled with loud, howling whines as shells from the big guns aboard Royal Navy warships out at sea whizzed overhead and exploded inland. I located Manning and insisted that he shared in the last few drops of gin. "Bertha didn't make it then eh, sir?" he asked.

"Well, she made it back – just about," I replied, "but the streets were too blocked with discarded stuff to get her through."

"The window for evacuation is closing fast, sir. If we don't leave soon…"

"Yes, you're quite right." I nodded. "I'm afraid there's nothing more to be done."

We joined the hobbling, rag-tag crowd of walking-wounded who were making their solemn way down the road into town.

The scene which met our eyes at the port was absolutely appalling; tens of thousands of people – like Margate on a bank holiday weekend – were gathered along the beaches and within the port's protective mole. Under an unbelievable barrage of covering fire from the Royal Navy, chaps were wading out – some of them up to their necks – to the waiting flotilla of small ships. Fortunately the weather remained fine and the sea calm.

I braced myself as I unzipped my fly and whipped-out the general. "Oh, Jesus Christ!" I gasped. It was what I imagined pissing white-hot molten magma would feel like. (I noticed that it was starting to whiff-up a bit too!)

Gonorrhoea is a sexually transmitted disease caused by infection with the bacterium *Neisseria gonorrhoeae* and has, since at least as far back as the sixteenth century, been commonly known as 'The Clap'. After an incubation period of two to ten days, infected men begin to experience pain while urinating (no bloody kidding!) and unpleasant discharge from the penis.

I still could not quite believe the turn of events and, frankly, I was bloody-well seething about it.

"Look out!" someone cried. "Incoming!"

"BANG!" Sods of soft sand, soggy seaweed and sodding sinewy stuff... (Confound my incessant alliteration – my apologies.) Anyway, I was covered in all sorts of unspeakable crap and peppered with tiny shards of hot metal. "You bastards!" I scowled, as the bloody Stuka screamed-off up the coast. It was then that I noticed my sergeant, lying face-down in the sand. "Manning?" I gasped. "Medic! I need a medic here – right now!"

The medic went to work with awesome British speed and skill and soon had young Manning's condition stabilised. "There's one bit of shrapnel that's best left where it is for now, sir," he reported as he finished his bandaging.

"He's going to be okay though?"

"Yeah, he'll be all right, sir."

"Oh, thank Christ for that," I sighed. "Thanks, Soldier."

"Not at all, sir," The medic smiled. "We'll let him rest-up for a bit; just keep an eye on him."

I spotted Colonel Brompton and was amazed to see that he was chatting with Farringdon and Dauphinois.

"Hugo!" the colonel exclaimed as he clapped eyes on me. "Bloody hell! I'm *so* glad that you made it, my boy!"

"I'm afraid that half of my platoon didn't, sir," I replied glumly.

"Hmmm," He frowned. "It's turned into an unmitigated bloody disaster."

"What on earth are you still doing here, Charles?" I asked Farringdon.

"Well, waiting for you of course." He shrugged.

"I threatened to have him shot and he *still* refused to leave!" said Brompton.

"My God, you really should've gone," I told Farringdon. "I mean, what if I hadn't made it back?"

"Don't be daft!" he grinned. "You're Captain H. J. bloody Poncenby, aren't you?"

"Ah, well, yes." I nodded. "Hmmm. And you, Dauphinois, why are *you* still here?"

"Why, we Frenchies know a sing or two about honour, *monsieur*," he said. "You saved zer lives of myself and my men; zere is no way zat I could leave wizout knowing zat you were okay."

"Then you're as daft as this silly bugger," I told him, nodding at Farringdon. "You both want your bloody heads knocked together!"

"How's that sergeant of yours?" asked Brompton.

"Yes, Manning's still with us, sir. He has some shrapnel which will have to stay-put until we get back to Blighty, but he's all in one piece at least."

"Good." He nodded. "He's bloody lucky; I thought that he was a goner."

"No," I said, "he wouldn't *dare* die without my permission, sir."

Despite my impassioned protests and claims of rude health, the colonel ordered me to get myself checked over by the MO and so I was rather compelled to do so.

"Right then," said the doc after his examination, "you've a big lump on the head; a gash in the cheek; an infected bullet-hole in the right shoulder; your left knee and both palms are deeply grazed; that knee would appear to be *very* swollen, too. There are various shrapnel wounds all over you – some of which will need a stitch or two – and you've got a raging dose of VD."

"Ugh!" I grimaced. "So it *is* the Clap then, eh?"

"Mm." He nodded. "Have you been poking it in these Continentals?"

"Well, yes, a bit," I said sheepishly. "Just the one." (*'Dirty little mare!'*)

"Regular intraurethral irrigations with Merbromin then, methinks." The doc smiled as he started to pop a couple of stitches in here and there.

"Good God!" I gasped. "What's wrong with sulphonamides?"

"Widespread resistance nowadays," he replied, shaking his head.

"But…antiseptic down the todger, Doc?" I cringed. "Strewth; it's bloody barbaric!"

"I *could* give you some penicillin, I suppose." He shrugged. "If you'd prefer that?"

"Hmmm, let me think now," I said. "A course of antibiotics or mercurochrome down the urethra? Call me mad, Doc, but the penicillin sounds very much more agreeable."

"Yes, I bet it bloody does!" he glowered disdainfully. "Try to be a bit more discerning as to where you stick it in future, eh?"

"Mm." I nodded as he finished-off the stitching and applied some dressings. "Abso-bloody-lutely!"

"Perhaps you ought to think about wearing something on it, eh?"

"Yes, yes, quite right," I agreed as I headed for the door.

"Left untreated, it rots the penis from the inside," he warned.

"Thanks, Doc," I said, beating a hasty retreat.

"It'll drop off, you know!" he called after me.

I re-joined the others and found Manning conscious but poorly looking (and sounding rather woozy on all the morphine he'd been given). "Oh, 'allo, sir," he drawled languidly from his stretcher. "Look at me, sir; I got blew up!"

"Yes." I nodded, looking down at him. "You bloody did, didn't you?"

"They bloody bombed me, sir!" he said indignantly, then added: "It's all right though, I didn't die."

"No, lad, very well done for not dying." I winked. "There's been far too much of that sort of thing going on lately."

On June 2, the British rear-guard (and a further 60,000 Frogs) abandoned France to the advancing Hun and evacuated. We had to wait until nightfall – it had become far too dangerous to carry out operations during the hours of daylight – but, shortly after sunset, Farringdon, Dauphinois, Manning, and myself gathered-up our few possessions and made our despondent way down onto the beach.

The acrid stink down by the sea was bloody fearsome; guts and severed limbs were scattered all over the place and bodies littered the shore and bobbed lazily up and down in the shallows; everywhere was the awful and overwhelming stench of death. With Manning's arm draped around my shoulder, we joined the long, snaking line of chaps who were wading out into the water. The sea looked black in the half light and, all around, dark and indistinct shapes bobbed about on the surface.

We were eventually picked up by a little 24-foot private fishing boat and taken out to deeper water, to a waiting merchant vessel, the MV *Lavender*. While a couple of merchant seamen helped Manning, Farringdon, and then Dauphinois aboard, I paused to take a last look across the devastation and to remember all of the valiant chaps whose lives had been lost.

"Your heroic sacrifices shall not have been in vain, lads," I vowed.

"Come on, Pongo," said one of the salts, "we're leaving!"

Every inch of *Lavender*'s deck space was already crammed-full of chaps, both British and French, all packed-in like sardines. There appeared to be a bit of a minor commotion going on nearby; a couple of scowling Tommies in disagreement with the ship's steward.

"What's going on here?" I demanded.

"This stupid tar, sir!" one of the soldiers glowered.

"We're supposed to take everyone's weapons off 'em, sir," said the steward. "We just can't get it out of his hands though."

"He's shell-shocked, you bloody idiot!" another chap seethed.

(The poor bugger in question had had most of his teeth blown out, but was still babbling to himself inanely, and was gripping his rifle so tightly that his fingers had turned white.)

"Look, it isn't loaded," I told the steward. "And he hasn't got any ammo. I think that he just needs something to hold onto, you know? We'll keep an eye on him."

The steward hesitated, unsure what to do. "All right then, sir," he said eventually. "You'll look after him?"

"Shan't leave his side." I winked.

Like most of the other chaps, the poor fellow was so bloody exhausted anyway that he simply laid down and went to sleep. I spent the next five hours being tossed about all over the show and vomited on but, considering what we'd all just been through, it was a small price to pay, to once again look upon Dover's gleaming, white cliffs and the lush, green grass of this majestic, sceptred isle.

It will be of interest (to all but the very most half-witted of dullards) to note that, amongst the equipment, which was left behind in France, were 85,000 vehicles (including 20,200 motorcycles) and 147,000 tons of fuel. Also dumped were 2,472 guns, 68,000 tons of ammunition, and some 377,000 tons of other supplies.

The original plan for Operation Dynamo had been to evacuate 30,000 BEFs over two days. Two further operations (*Aerial* and *Cycle*) were subsequently ordered and, by the early hours of June 4, 198,229 British soldiers and 139,997 Frenchies (a staggering 338,226 men, in all) had been rescued by Royal Navy destroyers, minesweepers and other ships, and aboard the 700 merchant marine and fishing boats, pleasure craft and RNLI lifeboats of the 'little ships of Dunkirk' flotilla. (Bloody unbelievable, what?)

Fate would soon carry me back across the Channel but, for the time being at least, I was safely home in Blighty. "Up yours, Hitler!" I scowled, glaring back across the shimmering sea. I went to step onto the quayside but managed to lose my footing. I slipped, did the splits, and damned-nearly tore all of my sodding stitches out. "Ooh, bugger!" I winced. "Damn this bloody war!"

Ingram Content Group UK Ltd.
Milton Keynes UK
UKHW010951070423
419773UK00012B/1019

9 781398 419537